MARION DANE BAUER

Killing Miss Kitty

and Other Sins

CLARION BOOKS
New York

For Jane Legwold,
with affection and gratitude

Clarion Books
a Houghton Mifflin Company imprint
215 Park Avenue South, New York, NY 10003
Copyright © 2007 by Marion Dane Bauer

The text was set in 13-point Clearface.

www.clarionbooks.com

Printed in the U.S.A.

Library of Congress Cataloging-in-Publication Data

Bauer, Marion Dane.
Killing Miss Kitty and other sins / by Marion Dane Bauer.
p. cm.
Summary: A series of five stories, loosely based on the author's
experiences growing up on the edge of a small industrial town in Illinois
in the 1950s, which touch on such diverse topics as race relations,
unwanted cats, confirmation in the Episcopal faith, and homosexuality.
ISBN-13: 978-0-618-69000-8
ISBN-10: 0-618-69000-X
[1. Interpersonal relations—Fiction. 2. Friendship—Fiction. 3. Family life—
Illinois—Fiction. 4. Illinois—History—20th century—Fiction.] I. Title.
PZ7.B3262Kil 2007
[Fic]—dc22   2006029590

MP 10 9 8 7 6 5 4 3 2 1

Acknowledgments

Thank you to those who read—and sometimes read and read and read—and supported me as I discovered these stories: Carolyn Coman, Norma Fox Mazer, and Louise Hawes (*especially* Carolyn and Norma and Louise), Laura Kvasnosky, Ellen Howard, Rita Williams Garcia, Sundee Frazer. Thanks to my partner, Ann Goddard, who has been part of everything I have written for the past twenty years. And my special appreciation to my editor, James Cross Giblin, who, as always, saw the book I intended and helped to shape my final vision.

Contents

A Word

My name is Claire, and these are my stories. The writer whose name is attached to this book might try to tell you they are hers, but you can't always believe writers.

These stories begin when I was still a girl and end when I was just beginning to learn what it means to be a woman. They occur from 1950 to 1955, a time very different from this one. And yet the girl I was then is not so different from the woman I am today. And for everything that was different about that time—rotary phones, bobby socks, legally sanctioned racism, a leering "innocence" about sexuality—more was the same. We all still longed for connection and found ourselves alone inside our own skins.

Friend of Liberty

I

I still remember the exact color of the sky the day I saw Dorinda for the first time. It was an early-summer blue, an expectant blue, the blue of a robin's egg. A few cottony clouds stood out against its wide canvas, and the smoke from the mill stack drifted overhead, as puffy and pristinely white as any cloud.

Sixth grade had ended just a couple of days before, and I was wandering the perimeter of my yard, making up stories in my head, as I loved to do.

When the strange girl appeared, I didn't yet know her name was Dorinda, of course. I didn't even know it was possible for such a girl to exist in our small northern Illinois town. All I knew was that, as I meandered along the edge of the deep woods that took up where our lawn left off, someone I'd never seen before had stepped out of the trees. Actually, she leapt out, jumping a rotting log that lay in her path and landing not more than three feet from where I stood.

I would have been more ready for the sudden appearance of an angel . . . or a troll. When the girl materialized directly in front of me, I stopped, utterly still, and stood gazing at her as though I'd just come upon a display of public art.

Her hair was braided in two long, thick braids that caused me to reach up and touch the empty space at the back of my own head where I had once had braids of equal heft and length. Her cheekbones were high and chiseled, her dark eyes filled with light. She wore a bright yellow sundress, starched and ironed, and white sandals that looked more suited for church than for tromping through the woods. And her skin glowed blue-black.

In that first startled examination, I thought everything about her fascinating. Mostly, though, it was her skin— the rich, dark color of it—that held me captive. This girl, this wondrously *colored* girl, couldn't have been more unexpected if she had dropped in from Mars. I wanted to touch her, just to see if she was real, and perhaps also to see if some of that delicious color might rub off onto my own paleness.

"Oh!" I said. And then again, "Oh!"

She made no response, just stood there, gleaming in the summer sunlight, and I finally managed to say, a bit more comprehensibly, "Where did you come from?"

She didn't answer, just ducked her head, the smallest flicker of a smile traveling across her mouth. Then she whirled around, so that her bright yellow skirt flew out behind her, and disappeared once more into the woods.

"Wait!" I called after her, but she didn't. And I stood for a long time, listening to her rustling retreat. I considered running after her into the dense stand of trees and seizing her arm to hold her back, but something—the unexpectedness of her arrival, perhaps, or maybe it was that richly glowing skin—frightened me just a bit, and so I did not.

Perhaps I should explain where we were, when this was, why this girl's appearance in my world startled me so deeply.

The place was the housing provided for the workers at the Lexington Cement Mill on the outskirts of Osborne, a small town in northern Illinois. If it hadn't been for the dusty, noisy mill, our surroundings would have been park-like, a few houses scattered on a wide expanse of lawn bordered on one side by the mill, on another by a farmer's cornfield—land rented from the mill—and on the two others by deep woods rising out of the Burgundy River Valley.

The year was 1950. That's important, that the year was 1950, the exact center of the twentieth century. Just recently, a British historian had said of our country, "America stands astride the world like a colossus." We in our small Midwestern town didn't actually stand astride much of anything, but if we had heard those words, we certainly would have agreed with them. We were Americans. We were the best!

To us, part of being "the best" in 1950 meant being

white. And we all were. Me. My family. Our neighbors. Everyone we knew. In 1950, not a single African American lived in the tri-city community of Lafayette-Pearson-Osborne.

Many years before, there had been a sign. It stood at the entrance to Lafayette, the town just across the Illinois River from Osborne, but it was taken to apply to all three of the closely tied communities. The sign said, very much to the point: NIGGER, DON'T LET THE SUN SET ON YOU IN THIS TOWN.

Blacks . . . African Americans—in that day they would have been politely called "colored" or "Negroes"—didn't eat in our restaurants, they didn't stay in our one hotel, they didn't attend our schools, and they certainly didn't buy or rent homes anywhere within the borders of our three towns. Negro entertainers might pass through as part of our community-concert series, but if they did, they sang or played their instruments or whatever else they might do for our entertainment and kept right on passing through.

My family's standards were not those of the town. I grew up knowing that the sign was wrong, that the discrimination that continued in the long years after the sign existed only as a memory—and then a rumor of a memory—was terribly wrong. But I also grew up believing that we—my mother, my father, my brother, and I—had nothing to do with that injustice. The town was at fault, not us. We were the ones who knew better.

I had seen colored people, of course. Not just the fascinating photographs of bare-breasted African women in the pages of *National Geographic*. We could see Negroes on the streets only fifteen miles away in the town of Tate, our county seat, and they were always evident when we took the long drive into Chicago. That they seemed to be concentrated in certain areas of the city didn't strike me as strange. I assumed they just liked it there.

That was how much I knew about African Americans in our deeply divided world.

And that was why this girl's arrival left me vibrating like a plucked harp. I had never seen a girl like her before—not close up, certainly not near my own house—and I had to tell someone about my discovery. Anyone. So that evening during supper at our Formica kitchen table, I casually dropped my bombshell into the conversation.

"I saw a Negro girl today," I said.

"You saw a *Negro* girl?" my mother repeated, rephrasing my statement as a question. Her expression was as unbelieving as if I'd announced that I'd just seen an elf.

"Where'd you see her?" My brother, Hugh, spoke without looking up from the pile of green beans on his plate, fresh from our garden, that he was lathering with butter.

"In our yard," I told him. "Just on the edge of the woods . . . over there." I pointed.

He snorted his usual contempt for my foolishness. Being thirteen to my eleven—along with being male— gave him lots of room for contempt. "*Sure,*" he said and took up a forkful of beans. "She probably took a little hike down here from Chicago."

I turned to my father, who said, "There's a Negro man here doing some troubleshooting at the mill. They brought him in from Chicago, I think." He shook his head, firmly, definitely. "My guess is he's staying over in Tate, but he can't have a child with him."

Hugh smirked at me from across the table. I could see what he was thinking. *Dumb Claire. As usual, you don't know what you're talking about.*

There was no point in looking to my mother again. She was a taciturn woman, little inclined to offer her opinion on much of anything, much less to defend my often embroidered version of reality.

I applied myself to buttering my own green beans, letting the matter melt away with the butter. Still, I knew that, however briefly I had seen her, the girl had been real. I hadn't made her up.

I made up lots of things. I entertained myself, day and night, making up things. But my dreams had never once included a colored girl emerging from the woods into our yard. They involved less surprising experiences, like my growing angel wings and long, flowing *curly* hair (a much blonder blond than my own straight taffy stuff), or waking up one morning three inches tall, or stepping through the mirror on my dressing table into that other, better room on the other side. That was the kind of stuff my dreams were made of, and I had always been savvy enough not to announce any of them at the kitchen table.

I spent the next several days pushing my way through the dense undergrowth of the surrounding woods in search of the girl. Each time I entered where I had last seen her and then struck out in one direction or another. I even made my way down the bluff to the banks of the Burgundy River. Yet I found no place where a girl of any color might be hiding out.

I was beginning to believe Hugh's teasing suggestion that she had walked here from Chicago . . . or at least over from Tate. Or, I told myself, she might be a runaway, in which case she had probably moved on by now.

She hadn't looked like a runaway, though. She'd looked like a girl who'd been brushed and combed and scrubbed and starched every day of her life. Being such a girl myself, I knew how little inclined she would be to run anywhere.

One hot afternoon, with the mutter of thunder growing closer and warning gusts turning the leaves on the trees to silver, I decided to give up my search. I'd gone farther than usual that day and had a good walk ahead of me to get home, so I hurried. I wanted to be out from under the trees before the storm arrived.

I knew I was nearly home when I reached a railroad track that radiated into the woods from the mill. My dad never let me go into the mill. It wasn't a place for a girl, he said. But this track extended out far enough to skirt the edge of our lawns, so I could walk there. It was a siding, a track where boxcars were shunted until they were needed for another load. I moved along quickly, stepping from wooden tie to wooden tie, beneath the sighing trees.

Still inside the screen of the woods, I was just about to

turn off the track, to step out from under the trees and head up the long hill to my house, when I came across something strange . . . a boxcar standing on the siding. There was, of course, nothing unusual about a boxcar's being there. Locomotives chuffed to and from the mill all the time, bringing coal to keep the kilns hot and carrying away the cement the mill produced, and cars were often shunted off to a siding to wait for the next load. But this one was different.

Windows had been cut into the sides of the car—proper windows with glass in them, framed by red-and-white-checked curtains. I'd seen thousands of boxcars rumbling and clanging alongside the mill, but not one had ever had windows, not to mention curtains.

The grass in the patch of ground beside the boxcar had actually been mowed, and a few toys were scattered about. One was a paddle ball, a small wooden paddle to which a ball was attached by a rubber band. I had the same thing at home, except the rubber band on mine was broken. I'd tried to tie it, but it kept coming untied as soon as I'd get a good volley going. There was a Margaret O'Brien paper doll book, too. Margaret O'Brien was a movie star, a girl only a few years older than I, and I adored her, but I had never had one of her paper doll books. And finally, there was a naked rubber baby doll. Its "skin" was a rich chocolate brown. It was the kind of doll I'd heard other kids refer to as a "nigger" baby, but the word wasn't allowed in my house.

I stood perfectly still, holding my breath, ignoring the

large raindrops threading their way through the canopy of trees and pelting my head. This had to be where the colored girl had come from. But how was such a thing possible? Though the mill stood on the very edge of town, it was still within the town limits. And I had never heard of anyone ignoring "the sign." However long ago it had been there, no one, neither colored nor white, had forgotten its message.

Just then, three things happened at once. A blast of thunder exploded right over my head; the sky opened and dropped its load of water; and a girl catapulted from the boxcar, leaping past the makeshift wooden steps that had been set before the sliding door, and tore around to pick up the scattered toys. She went for the brown doll first, though since it was made of rubber and completely undressed, the rain clearly would not have hurt it. It wasn't until she had everything tucked under one arm that she stopped, directly in front of me.

"Who are you?" she asked. Her dress—today she was wearing a pink one with puffy sleeves and violets sprinkled about—was already soaked and clinging to her skinny frame. She was my size, so I took her to be my age, but she might have been an adult, even a teacher, from the way she spoke. Her tone made me feel as though I had appeared where I didn't belong and was about to get a good scolding.

"I'm Claire," I replied. "You saw me the other day. I live . . ." But my voice failed me, so I just pointed toward the open expanse of lawn that could be glimpsed through the trees behind me. My house wasn't far, just up a hill, maybe a long city block from where I stood. I had never seen this boxcar before, though, because the tracks were both closer in to the mill than I usually traveled and entirely enclosed by trees.

"What are you doing here?" she said. Again, she wasn't exactly rude; she just spoke in that grown-up-in-charge manner.

I could have asked her the same thing. After all, I had lived here, at number 3 Trenton Avenue, next to the mill, next to the cornfield, next to the woods, for nearly my entire life. The part that hadn't been spent here had been spent at 19 Lexington Avenue on the other side of the cornfield where a double row of smaller company houses stood facing one another across a red slag street. And this girl, who was questioning me in such an imperious way, had just emerged from a boxcar! But something about her tone made me feel obligated to answer.

"I . . . I . . ." And then because I couldn't think of anything else to say, I blurted out the truth, "I was looking for you."

"Well," the girl replied, one fist cocked on a narrow hip. "Here I am." The water poured down her face and dripped off her bent elbow. "So I guess you'd best come inside out of the rain."

By that time there was little point in coming in out of the rain. We were both drenched to the skin—I in my shorts and sleeveless plaid blouse, the girl in her pretty pink dress. But I climbed the steps into the boxcar willingly, trying to shear the water off my skin with my hands even as the heavy rain continued to drench me.

Inside, I stopped, amazed. This wasn't just a boxcar. It was a real home. A tiny cabin set on wheels with a stove, icebox, and sink, an easy chair, a couch, and a wooden kitchen table with two chairs. The other end of the car had been partitioned off into a separate room, and through the open door I could see a neatly made bed. The rain drummed loudly on the roof, but the racket only served to make the place feel cozier.

I stared and stared, taking in everything—the paper napkins in their plastic holder on the table, the hand-crocheted throw folded at the end of the couch, the braided rugs on the floor.

"Why don't you take a picture?" the girl finally said. "It'll last longer."

It's exactly what one of the girls at school might have said to me—actually, *had* said, on more than one occasion, whenever I stood too long, lost in my own thoughts. Instantly, I felt heat climb up my neck and set my cheeks on fire. "Sorry! I didn't mean . . . it's just that I . . . I've never known anybody who lived in a boxcar before." And thinking of *The Boxcar Children,* a book about orphans who take refuge in a boxcar, I added, "Are you alone? Don't you have somebody to take care of you?"

The girl laughed, and her laughter was warm, lacking any trace of mockery, so I relaxed a little. "Of course I do," she said. "My daddy's here doing some work at the mill. He's the best troubleshooter they've got, you know?

That's why they asked him to come here in spite of . . ." She stopped without saying in spite of what, though, of course, I knew. In spite of the fact that people like her daddy weren't welcome in our town.

"Do you have a mother?" I asked, those orphans still stuck in my head.

"What do you think?" Her tone was incredulous, even amused. "My mama's a teacher. She had to stay back in Chicago to teach summer school. No way could she get out of it this time."

I nodded. Instead of asking something else foolish, I turned slowly, taking in everything once more. The dishes stacked neatly in the doorless cupboard. The radio on the counter. Apparently, the boxcar was even hooked up to electricity! The magazines on the table next to the couch. *Popular Science* and *The Saturday Evening Post*. We got those magazines at my house, too. And back to the hand-crocheted throw again. I could see now that it covered a bed pillow. Someone must sleep on the couch at night.

I completed my circle and faced the girl again. Her dark hair had a soft, fuzzy look, despite being pulled very firmly into the two long braids, and raindrops glittered on the surface. Her wet skin looked polished.

"My name's Dorinda," the girl said, finally. "Dorinda Smith. Is that big gray house yours? The one I saw you near?"

I nodded once more. "I'm Claire Davis. My dad works at the mill. And my mom's a teacher, too. She teaches

12

kindergarten, but not during the summer." Even as I spoke, I was thinking, *Smith! Her name is Smith! Could anything be more ordinary?* Though there was certainly nothing common about the name Dorinda. And I still found myself having to clasp my hands behind my back to prevent them from reaching out of their own accord and touching her.

Dorinda got a towel out of a cupboard for herself and another for me. We both began drying our arms and legs, our hair.

When we were as dry as we could get, standing there in our sodden clothes, we continued staring at one another until I finally said, "I still don't understand. What are you doing *here?*" I waved my hand, a bit feebly, to indicate our surroundings.

"Here, living in a boxcar, you mean?" Dorinda asked, taking both of our towels and laying them over the backs of the wooden chairs at the kitchen table to dry. "Or here, in this town that"—her manner of speaking suddenly changed—"don't allow no sun to set on no *niggers.*"

She leaned heavily on the word *niggers,* and I flinched. So she knew about the sign, though it had been gone longer than either of us had been alive. But then I assumed most people in Illinois—probably especially most colored people—knew about the sign exactly the way I did. The memory of it seemed to live in the air around these three communities.

There was something about her change of speech that bothered me, too. She might have been making fun of me, but I wasn't sure. "Both, I guess," I said, my voice uncertain and low. But then I added, more strongly, "I didn't use *that word*, though."

"You want points for that? For not using *that word?*"

My face burned, and I didn't reply. This girl—Dorinda—seemed to have a way of turning everything upside down.

But then she surprised me by ducking her head and saying, "Sorry. I really didn't mean—" She stopped, started up again. "I don't like it, hiding out here. I don't like this stupid town, either. But Mama said I had to come, so . . ."—she heaved a huge sigh that brought her shoulders practically to her ears before dropping them again—"I'm here."

"Why . . ." *Why don't you like this town?* I was going to ask. But I realized before I spoke that it would be a truly stupid question. So I asked instead, "Why did they make you come?"

"Because they thought I'd be safer here. Glory! I'm so safe some days, I think I might die of it!"

"Safe from what?"

"Polio." Dorinda rolled her eyes as though polio were no big deal. "A kid in our apartment building got it, and one across the street, too, so Mama was worried. She said sending me here with Daddy would be the best way to keep me safe."

Polio! I stepped back. People—especially kids, it seemed—were getting polio all over the country. "Infantile paralysis," it was called, and some people died of it. And some who didn't die couldn't walk anymore once they were well, like President Roosevelt, who'd been our president before Truman. Sometimes they couldn't even breathe without a machine called an iron lung! These hot summer months were the worst for it. What if this girl was carrying polio germs from Chicago?

"No one at the mill even knows I'm here with Daddy," she went on. "They fixed up this boxcar just for him so he wouldn't have to drive back and forth to Tate. I'm supposed to lie low during the day so nobody sees me." She narrowed her eyes and glared at me. "You won't tell, will you?"

"I won't tell. Cross my heart and hope to die. Stick a needle in my eye!" I made a cross over my heart and raised my right hand.

I was still wondering about Dorinda's age. "Are you going into seventh grade, too?" I asked, taking the direct approach.

She nodded. That meant, I figured, she was probably twelve to my eleven, as I was at the young end of my class.

But with that exchange, the conversation stumbled to a halt—as though having established our rank in school, nothing more remained to be said.

"You like dolls?" I asked finally, nodding toward the rubber baby doll she had dropped onto the couch along with the rest of the toys she had rescued.

She lifted one shoulder in a half-shrug. "Do you?"

"Yeah," I admitted. "But I never play baby dolls like little kids do."

Dorinda frowned. "What do you do with them, then?"

"I make up stories and use the dolls to act them out. I've always liked—" But just then the mill whistle blew, a hoarse, throaty bellow, followed by another peal of thunder. The commotion cut me off midsentence. The whistle blew for every change of shift, and its blowing now meant that it was four-thirty and that my dad—and the other men who worked at the mill—would soon be walking home.

The effect of the noise on Dorinda was instantaneous and dramatic. Her hands flew to cover her mouth. "You gotta go! You can't stay here anymore. My daddy—" She didn't finish, just put her hands on my shoulders, turned me around, and propelled me toward the door. She might have been a skinny thing, but she was plenty strong.

For an instant, I teetered on the edge of the doorway at the top of the roughly constructed wooden steps. Then the next thing I knew, I was standing in the middle of the cut grass in front of the boxcar getting soaked all over again. The door had slid closed behind me. The rain still hammered, and the trees surrounding the clearing bowed in the wind, straightened, then bowed again.

"Well," I said, under my breath, though Dorinda probably couldn't have heard me over the sounds of the storm even if I had shouted. "It was nice meeting you, too."

Feeling rather sorry for myself, I started toward my house. Not only was I soaked, but I had been thoroughly rejected . . . and by a *colored* girl. I'd been nice to her, hadn't I? And I'd promised I wouldn't tell anyone she was here, so what would have been so terrible about Dorinda's father's coming home and finding me visiting? Unless he didn't like whites. But that wasn't possible, was it? Everybody liked whites.

The door of the boxcar rumbled open behind me, and a voice called out, "Will you come back tomorrow? When our daddies are at work, I mean?"

I glanced over my shoulder. Dorinda stood framed in the doorway, her expression open and hopeful, her pretty pink dress still limp and clinging to her skinny frame. I shrugged, turning my palms out in a kind of "Who knows?" gesture. I didn't want her to think I was so desperate for friends that I'd be back the next day after she'd practically thrown me out into the storm. The truth was, though, I *was* pretty desperate. In the mill housing, there were lots of boys near my brother's age for him to hang around with, but no girls for me. My steady playmates, the mill superintendent's daughters, had moved the past winter when their father was given a job as superintendent over all the Lexington Mills. So after the shrug, I nodded. I kept the nod small, though, so as not to seem too eager.

If Dorinda noticed any lack of enthusiasm on my part, she didn't show it. "Bring some dolls," she called cheerfully. "I want to hear one of your stories."

I gave her a wave and turned away again, ducking my head against the driving rain . . . though that only made the water run down inside my collar. Would I be back? Of course I would be. Nothing could have kept me—or my dolls—away.

II

"What are their names?" Dorinda held up the Campbell kid twins, dolls made to resemble the round-faced boy and girl with page-boy bobs used to advertise Campbell's soup.

"He's Keith. She's Kate." I pulled my other set of twin dolls from the grocery bag I'd brought everything in. "And here's Patsy and Pansy." Patsy wore a red-checked sundress. Pansy's dress was blue-checked. All four of the dolls were made of a hard substance that was basically papier-mâché, as most dolls were then, with molded hair and painted-on eyes.

"You can take Keith," Dorinda said, thrusting him into my hands and keeping Kate. "I don't like boys. And I'll take her." She reached for Pansy, my favorite of the girl twins.

The truth was I preferred the girl dolls, too, and I thought it would have been nice for Dorinda to wait to see which dolls I wanted to give her rather than taking over that way. But since I'd left her the day before, I'd thought of nothing else besides the fact that I had someone to play out a new story with, so I took Keith and let Pansy go.

"Okay." Dorinda settled down on the braided rug in front of the couch with Kate and Pansy in front of her. "Start making up a story," she commanded.

I tamped down the irritated response that wanted to fly from my lips and began, "Well, they're all orphans. And they live in an orphanage . . . a cruel orphanage, where they don't get enough to eat, and they have to scrub floors all day long."

"Must be the cleanest floors in town," Dorinda grumbled. "All those kids scrubbing all the time." But she reached under the sink and came out with a rag from which she tore small pieces, one for each doll, and the four dolls set to scrubbing.

I stood the Keith doll up. "But Keith has an idea!" I said.

"Why does it have to be the boy who has the idea?" Dorinda fired back. "Girls get ideas, too."

"Okay. Patsy has an idea!" And I stood up the Patsy doll in her red-checked dress. "Let's run away from this awful place."

"That's the best idea ever," Pansy replied in Dorinda's husky voice.

And we were off . . .

We played all morning, and when the mill whistle blew at noon, I didn't wait to be evicted from the boxcar. I immediately packed the dolls up in the grocery bag and hurried down the wooden steps to the grass.

"Will you come back?" Dorinda asked, standing in the open doorway. "After lunch, will you bring your dolls and come again?"

"Sure," I agreed, feeling magnanimous. Dorinda must be pretty lonely, sitting around the boxcar all day with nothing to do but wait for her father to come home. Besides, even if she was a bit bossy, I liked anyone who liked my stories.

So that was the way we passed the summer days. I went to Dorinda's first thing in the morning after our dads were off to work, left for the noon hour, and went back again until the four-thirty whistle blew. When my mother asked where I disappeared to every day, I said, in an offhanded manner, "I'm building a village for my dolls in the woods." And that gave me the idea to really do it.

So we moved from the boxcar a short distance into the woods, where we found a grassy clearing, lots of dropped twigs to use for building houses, a trickling stream that just begged to be dammed to form a doll-sized lake, woodland blossoms to decorate our dolls' tables, and even a fallen tree to wall ourselves and our small community off with in case someone came walking by. I couldn't remember when I'd had so much fun. For every idea I had, Dorinda had another, and the complexity of our dolls' personalities and lives grew day by day.

I began to bring other dolls, too, such as the Toni doll, my most recent acquisition. She had nylon hair—all the best and most exciting new products were made out of nylon in 1950—and you could wet it with a permanent solution (that was actually sugar water) and set it. Then when it dried, you had . . . well, what you really had were ugly, stiff curls, so mostly we didn't mess with setting the Toni doll's hair.

And I brought my Kewpie doll, too. She was the same size as the others, about ten inches, but she had a more infantile look, so she was the baby sister. Both Dorinda and I, we discovered, had always wanted a baby sister.

On weekends, Dorinda and her dad usually made the trek back to Chicago, but even when they didn't, she couldn't count on him to be working the usual hours, so our play had to stop. But while we were apart, I began to think about how much fun it would be to bring Dorinda to *my* house to play. I got a new doll every year—it was always the centerpiece of my Christmas—so I had dolls she hadn't even seen.

Finally, an opportunity came. My mother announced that she was going into town for her book club meeting, which always included lunch, and Hugh took off for the day to ride his bike to a distant park with a friend. So I arrived at the boxcar without my usual sack of dolls and said, casually, "I thought we'd play at my house this morning." Then I held my breath, waiting to see what Dorinda would say.

"Really?" she asked. She stood in the wide doorway, her head tipped to one side, examining me quizzically. "Do you mean it?" And before I could assure her that I did, she added, "I'm supposed to stay right here. My daddy said."

"But," I wheedled, "you've been playing with me, and you're not supposed to be doing that, either. So what's the difference if you come to my house this one time? You can be back here before your father gets off for lunch. And nobody will see you. My dad's at the mill, and my mom and my brother are both gone, so we'll have the house all to ourselves."

Obedience and desire battled in Dorinda's brown eyes, and after only a few seconds, desire won. "Okay," she said.

"But we've got to watch the clock. We can't wait for the whistle to blow before I go back. Daddy might get here before me."

And so we walked to the edge of the woods. I paused for a few self-important seconds, holding Dorinda back inside the shelter of the trees to make sure no one from any of the other houses was out and about. Finding the coast clear, I motioned her forward, and we walked quickly up the steep hill to my two-story frame house. We passed through the small enclosed entry porch and into the kitchen.

"Wow!" Dorinda said, stopping to stare. "It's so big!"

I looked around, noticing for the first time that it *was* a big kitchen, wide and sunny with yellow walls that intensified the light flowing in through the windows. "Is your kitchen small?" I asked. "Back home in Chicago, I mean?"

She laughed, a single, short burst of breath. "You could fit my mama's kitchen in here three times . . . maybe four."

I led the way through the dining room and into the long living room that ran the width of the house. The living room had a fireplace flanked by glassed-in bookshelves at one end. Dorinda moved immediately to the bookshelves to study the titles. Then she turned to take in the whole room. "You could just about fit our whole apartment in here," she said.

"Why don't you get a bigger apartment?" I asked, genuinely bewildered. After all, they couldn't be poor. Her father worked for the cement mill just the way my dad did, and her mother was a teacher, exactly the same as my mother. The clothes she wore were a lot nicer than mine, too.

Again, that abrupt, almost rude laugh. "Don't you know? Colored folks have to take what we can get. If we were white, Daddy says that for the same money we pay for our tiny apartment we could have one with lots of space and one of those men in a fancy uniform guarding the front door. Or maybe we could even have a house."

I flushed. I should have been prepared for the idea of racism in the north. After all, I'd been born into the midst of such a reality. But nonetheless, I was shocked to discover that the mere color of someone's skin could make the world so unfair. And I didn't understand why discovering that it was so made *me* feel ashamed, as though I ought to apologize.

I said nothing, though, and Dorinda followed me up the stairs and down the hallway to my bedroom. My room was small, with a sloping ceiling. It was also intensely pink. I'd painted it myself.

Miss Kitty, our gray tabby, was stretched out asleep at the foot of my bed. When Dorinda stroked her, the cat rose, jumped down to the floor and stalked out of the room, the tip of her tail twitching in irritation.

"Don't mind her," I told Dorinda. "She doesn't like anybody. Not even me, and I'm the one who feeds her." Or at least, I was the one who fed her when I remembered to do it.

But Dorinda's attention had already turned from the crabby cat to the rest of my dolls, especially one of them.

"Oh!" she said, lifting the doll from the small chair she sat in beneath the window. "Isn't she beautiful?"

I looked. Was she? I'd never thought so especially, though her "skin" was pale, her cheeks rosy, and she wore a pink satin coat and bonnet over her white dress and slip. Her hair was "real"—not the shining nylon of the Toni doll but some softer, duller brown stuff—and her eyes opened and closed. She had been a gift one Christmas from an aunt whom I rarely saw, and I didn't play with her much. She was too big, nearly twice as big as any of the other dolls, and yet she was clearly meant to be a baby, so she didn't fit in with my stories.

"Her name is Prudy," I told Dorinda. And then, as Dorinda went on talking to and cuddling the doll, I found myself adding, almost surprising myself, "Do you want her? You can have her . . . to keep, I mean."

Dorinda looked down at the doll, long and hard. Prudy's peaches-and-cream skin looked somehow sickly against Dorinda's elegantly long dark fingers. She tipped Prudy back so that her blue eyes snapped closed with a little *clunk.* She lifted the doll up, and the eyes snapped open again. Then, finally, she looked at me.

"Really?" she asked. And then, with a scowl, "Why?"

Why? What could I say? Because it's unfair that your family has to live in a crummy apartment just because you're Negro? It was, but was that why I had offered her the doll? Or was it because it had been forever since I'd had a friend to play with, and I was grateful she was there? Or because all the other girls I knew who were our age thought they were too old to play with dolls, even if the only thing we were using them for was making up stories?

I shrugged. "I don't know. I just thought you might like to have her."

Dorinda's scowl deepened. "You think I don't have any dolls of my own? So you gotta give me yours?"

I didn't know what to say. I knew she had her own dolls. I'd seen one of them the first day. And I'd just wanted to do something nice.

"No," I said. "I don't think that. I don't think anything. I just never liked that old doll very much, and I thought you did, so I figured you might as well have her. But if you don't want her, that's perfectly all right." I could hear my own voice. I sounded self-righteous, snotty. I turned away.

Silence vibrated in the room—silence louder than any noise either of us was capable of making. And I thought, *Now she won't want to play with me anymore.*

Dorinda broke the quiet. "You don't like her?" I turned to see that she was smiling. Clearly she had decided to ignore my tone, even to ignore the sniff of condescension in my gift. "You *really* don't like her?"

I nodded, holding my breath.

"Well, I love her!" She pulled the doll to her chest in an extravagant hug. "Thank you!" But then, as quickly as her smile had come, it faded, and she added, "But I can't take her home, you know. My daddy would want to know where I got her."

"Well," I said, relief flooding me—she wasn't offended, after all!—"by the time you and your daddy go back home, we'll figure something out."

Dorinda looked at me for a long moment, then nodded, satisfied, apparently assuming I would be able to figure something out. I couldn't help wondering, though, where she came by such faith in me.

"Anyway," Dorinda said, "I can play with her for now."

We settled back into our play, deciding, after removing the babyish bonnet, that Prudy would be the dolls' mother. She'd been sent to jail for stealing bread to feed her children, and now she was out, searching everywhere for them.

The search took the mother doll into my clothes closet. "What's this?" Dorinda asked, backing into the room. She held up a red, white, and blue Uncle Sam–style hat I'd made by covering an oatmeal box with construction paper.

"That's for the Fourth of July parade," I told her. "I'm going to be Liberty. I'll wear that hat and a red shirt and my blue shorts with white stars pinned on them." I explained how on the afternoon of the Fourth, the kids in town dressed up in patriotic costumes and decorated their bikes and scooters and wagons. Then they walked or rode around the perimeter of the town park in a parade.

"A parade?" Dorinda repeated. The idea seemed to strike her with awe.

"Just a little one. The band from the grade school marches and plays. They sound awful, all screechy and off time, but still it's fun. The mayor gives out prizes for the best-decorated bike and the best costume . . . things like that."

"Ohhh!" Dorinda said, with a profound exhalation of breath. "I've always wanted to be in a parade!" And sitting there, with the mama doll that was really a baby cuddled in her lap and some longing I couldn't have named bright in her eyes, she suddenly, for the first time, seemed to be younger than I. Younger in hope, somehow. Like a little kid waiting for Santa Claus.

I was amazed at such an all-believing hope in a girl who had already come to terms with a world where apartments are meted out according to the color of a person's skin. So amazed that, despite everything I knew, I said, "Well . . . do you want to come with me? We could make you a Liberty costume, too."

For a moment she hesitated, as though she might actually say yes, and I found myself holding my breath. But then, abruptly, she turned away. "My daddy'd blister my behind if I ever showed my face in this town. You know that."

"Yes," I said, filled with a curious mixture of disappointment and relief. "I know that."

Dorinda put the hat for my costume back in the closet, and we dropped the matter entirely, but our play for the rest of the morning was stiff, forced in a way it had never been before. What must it be like, I wondered, to be excluded from a whole town, even from a parade meant to celebrate liberty?

But I didn't ask.

III

About three days later, while we were playing in our clearing in the woods, Dorinda said, apropos of nothing we were doing or talking about, "I'm tired of it!"

"Tired of what?" I asked, startled. Didn't she like the story I was weaving? I thought it incredibly sad. After all, the baby sister was just about to die of polio.

"Tired of doing every single thing my daddy says," Dorinda replied.

I sat back on the grass, relieved. "Like staying hidden away in the boxcar all the time?"

"Yeah. And like missing all the fun on the Fourth of July."

I stared at her. What was she hatching? "Didn't you say your daddy would—"

"That he'd blister my behind if I showed my face in this town? Yeah. That's what I said."

"But you want to do it anyway? You want to go to the parade?"

She wiped her nose abruptly with the back of her hand. "He just told me that since the Fourth is on a Tuesday— practically the middle of the week—we can't go home. So he's going to work that day. The whole danged day. If he's at the mill, how's he going to know where my face shows itself?"

"But . . . but . . ." How could I say it? She knew about the sign. She'd mentioned it before.

Dorinda interrupted my faltering objections. "Tell me," she said. "What time's the parade?"

"Two o'clock."

"Two o'clock in the afternoon. Right?"

"Right." And then, suddenly, I understood where she was going. *Don't let the sun set on you in this town! Don't let the sun set on you!*

What could anyone do? Long before Independence Day was over, Dorinda would have disappeared back into her tidy little boxcar home. So she wouldn't be breaking any laws, written or unwritten. Not breaking them so that anyone knew about it, anyway. And since no one in town would have any idea who she was or where she had come from, who could tell her father anything?

I began to smile, enjoying the idea. "So," I said. "Should we make you a Liberty costume?"

"Of course!" She clapped her hands.

"And if anyone asks, if they say anything at all, I'll just tell them—" I came to a halt. What would I tell them?

"You just say I'm your cousin, visiting from Chicago!"

I stared at Dorinda. Her dark eyes danced. I began to giggle. Then she giggled, too.

The next thing I knew, we were rolling around in the grass, clutching our knees and laughing hysterically.

This was going to be best Fourth of July ever!

Once she'd made up her mind to disobey her father, Dorinda didn't seem to worry about another thing. We made her a hat out of construction paper pasted to an oatmeal box, like mine, and pinned white stars onto a blue shirt of hers. I loaned her some red shorts. We kept her costume in my bedroom closet, since there was no place in her boxcar to hide anything.

As the day approached, though, I found myself making up things to worry about, like: Would Hugh spoil everything by deciding to go to the parade with me? What would he think of Dorinda if he did? What would he say about her to our parents? It wasn't that I thought they would object to my playing with a Negro girl. They weren't like that. But I had a pretty strong feeling the secrecy with which I'd been doing it wouldn't be appreciated.

And what if my parents themselves decided to drive into town to watch the parade?

Or maybe Dorinda's father would change his mind at the last minute and not work on the Fourth. Then all of our preparations would be for nothing.

But none of that happened. On the morning of the Fourth, Hugh went down to the Burgundy River with a friend. They had a homemade boat tethered there that they liked to mess around in. My mother bustled about her sunny kitchen, assembling a picnic for later that evening when we were all going out to the park in Lafayette to watch the fireworks. Dad sat in the living room in his favorite chair, reading and listening to *Oklahoma!* on his console radio/record player. And when I arrived at the boxcar in the woods shortly after lunch, Dorinda's father was at the mill where he was supposed to be.

I gave Dorinda her costume, and she hurried into it.

Then she brought out something I hadn't expected. Two large white signs hanging on strings so they could be worn around our necks. One said LIBERTY. The other said FRIEND OF LIBERTY.

"Oh, what a great idea!" I said, reaching for the LIBERTY sign.

Dorinda pulled it back and thrust FRIEND OF LIBERTY at me instead.

I opened my mouth to object. After all, being Liberty had been my idea to start with. But one look at her face warned me. She had the same look she'd had back when she'd decided how the dolls were to be parceled out. I shrugged—I was used to following her dictates by now—and dropped FRIEND OF LIBERTY over my head, positioning it across my chest.

Then I looked at Dorinda—really looked at her, at her dark face above her bold sign—and a small shiver traveled from my scalp all the way down my spine. Was this a good idea?

But whether it was a good idea or not, Dorinda had already stepped through the boxcar door and out into the shining day. "Come on!" she called back cheerfully, and so I did.

The walk along Osborne's Main Street to the park where the festivities were to be held was little more than a mile, and though it was a walk I'd made often and easily—my school wasn't far from the park—it had never seemed longer than it did that bright July afternoon. Every single car that bumped by on the brick street slowed as it approached . . . so the people inside could gawk, I knew. A man standing in the doorway of one of the taverns stepped out onto the sidewalk to stare after us. Even a mangy yellow dog trailed us for a while, sniffing, as though our footsteps left some kind of exotic scent.

"Haven't you ever seen a colored girl before?" I wanted to shout at the entire town of Osborne, but if Dorinda noticed that her presence was causing consternation, she didn't show it. She walked perfectly erect, gazing curiously at the town, though I could see little that deserved notice. A string of taverns. A couple of grocery stores. A drug store. A movie theater. One dress shop. Some brick city-office buildings that included the library in an upstairs room. The school. And then, as we turned off Main Street toward the park, small frame houses on neatly trimmed, square lawns. Osborne looked pretty much like every other small Midwestern town as far as I could see.

"Is this it?" Dorinda asked when we arrived, finally, at the edge of the park. "Is this the parade?"

I could tell she was disappointed.

I looked around at the motley collection of kids holding tiny flags; at the bicycles with red, white, and blue crepe paper woven through the spokes; at the band that seemed to be mostly tubas. "Well," I said. "There might be a few more coming, but I'd guess this is pretty much it. I told you a parade in Osborne isn't a big deal."

As if to emphasize my point, a boy blared out a squawk-
ing *oom-pah-pah* on his tuba.

But if Dorinda was disappointed, she refused to show
it. "Okay," she said. "Let's go." And she stepped smartly
into the ragged line that was forming, preparing to circle
the park.

Suddenly self-conscious, I looked around to see if anyone there would know me, but all the rest of the kids in
the parade seemed to be younger than we were. Even the
summer before, I now remembered, I had been the only
one there from my grade. Obviously, kids my age thought
Fourth of July parades—at least the kiddie variety held in
Osborne—were as dumb as dolls. I smiled, relieved.

But was I, I asked myself, relieved because I didn't want
to be seen with Dorinda? The very thought made me step
closer to her and hook my arm through hers. After all,
wasn't I Liberty's friend?

Dorinda shook me off with a small, impatient gesture. I
shrugged, but kept close by her side. Maybe she had forgotten what our signs said.

Just then, the band started up, playing something that
was almost "America the Beautiful," and we all started
off. We hadn't walked more than a few feet, though, when
I noticed that a group of adults standing along the side
were whispering among themselves and staring . . . at
Dorinda, of course.

"How do you like being in a parade?" I asked her, trying
to keep her attention from the gawkers.

"I like it just fine," Dorinda replied, her words crisp,

bitten off sharply. But though she walked with her back erect and her chin high, her eyes had lost their usual lively sparkle. Clearly, despite my earlier disclaimers, Dorinda's idea of a parade hadn't come from the little town of Osborne. It was also clear she wasn't enjoying the attention she was getting.

Why hadn't we thought about that? Why hadn't *I* thought about it? If you are going to break a rule in front of a whole town, people are going to whisper and stare.

A tiny GI walked in front of us, holding his mother's hand. He kept gaping over his shoulder at Dorinda. Every time he turned to look, he stumbled, and his mother had to hold his arm high to keep him on his feet and moving forward. Finally, she glanced back to see what was distracting him. When she saw, she stumbled, too.

I smiled sweetly, and the mother whipped back around, raising the little soldier's hand even higher until he had to run along, his feet barely touching the ground while his mother put distance between us.

Dorinda's expression had gone still as stone.

Worse than the starers, though, were the ones who looked away, as if Dorinda's presence were in bad taste somehow and they were embarrassed. And then there was the group of mothers who stood with their mouths gaping so wide I could practically see which ones still had their tonsils.

"Where did that darkie come from?" one woman asked.

"What does she think she's doing here?" huffed another.

"Look, Mama," a little girl with sandy curls cried in a high, piping voice, pointing. "There's a nigger!"

No one bothered to correct her.

I glanced at Dorinda. *Aren't they dumb?* I wanted to say.

But if Dorinda had heard the comments, she gave no sign. She just kept walking, her back ramrod straight, her Uncle Sam–style hat balanced perfectly on her head.

The sun blared from an enameled sky. Sweat ran down between my shoulder blades. I could see the judges—the mayor and the city clerk—just ahead. Maybe they would appreciate our small pageant. Maybe they would give us a ribbon. Even an honorable mention would be nice. The blue ribbons, I knew, usually went to the miniature Uncle Sams and Betsy Rosses, because they were so cute.

But we had barely come even with Mayor Kowalski, a round man with a fringe of white hair and a pink face, when a hand reached into the stream of marchers, clamped onto Dorinda's shoulder, and pulled her out of line. It was the city clerk. He twisted Dorinda around and presented her to the mayor, whose pink face had begun to turn purple.

I stopped walking. Everyone behind us did, too. Had I known this was going to happen? Was this why I'd been afraid? What should I do?

"What in the hell," the mayor said, bending over Dorinda and speaking out of the side of his mouth, but quite audibly nonetheless, "do you think you're doing here, girl?"

"Walking in the parade, sir," Dorinda answered. She said it simply, her voice low, but, like the mayor's, perfectly audible to anyone who stood near. Even the tubas had stopped playing now, and the entire procession seemed to have stumbled to a halt.

The city clerk joined the interrogation. "Where did you come from?" he demanded. He gave Dorinda's shoulder a little shake and hunched over her in a way that reminded me of a vulture over its prey.

For all the bravado of her first response, Dorinda looked incredibly small before the looming men. In fact, I could have sworn she was shrinking. She bowed her head, and her red, white, and blue oatmeal box hat tumbled to the ground.

I couldn't stand it. Not for another minute. I stepped forward and snatched Dorinda's hat from the grass. "She's my cousin," I announced, "my cousin visiting from Chicago." And when the men turned their astonished stares on me, I added, "But you don't need to worry. She'll be gone long before the sun sets on this town."

I spoke in a normal voice, but my words might have been a thunderclap for the response they got. The other adults who had been standing nearby, watching this spectacle, drew back. The city clerk pulled himself upright with a jerk. The mayor's face seemed to grow larger, rounder, darker, as though it might be about to explode. The two men stared at Dorinda's LIBERTY sign and at my FRIEND OF LIBERTY. They both opened their mouths, I assume to protest, but nothing came out of either one.

And before either man could gather himself enough to speak, Dorinda broke free of the city clerk's grasp and ran. No one was holding onto me, so I followed close on her heels.

We were at least two blocks away before Dorinda finally stopped running. She bent over, her hands on her knees, puffing for breath. I stopped beside her, breathing hard, too, and waited for the laughter I was sure would come next.

Dorinda burst into tears.

I waited a few beats for the tears to dissolve into giggles or at least for the crying to stop. When neither happened, I laid a tentative hand on Dorinda's shoulder. Beneath my palm, her bones felt as delicate as eggshells, as unyielding as stone. "I'm sorry," I said. But I didn't know whom I was apologizing for. For the mayor and the city clerk? For my whole town?

For myself . . . because I was white?

"I think we should go home," I said.

Liberty straightened slowly, scrubbing at her wet cheeks with both palms. "It ain't no home of mine," she said.

IV

We walked in silence back along the main street we had traveled up so boldly.

"Well," I said finally, trying to resurrect something of our original good feeling. "Now you've seen Osborne."

Dorinda gave no response.

A car approached. The driver, an older woman I didn't

37

recognize, slowed, obviously to stare. I stuck out my tongue, and she stepped on the gas.

The July sun rode high in the sky. Except for that one car, the town seemed to be deserted. Apparently, most people who were out and about were at the parade or off visiting family for the holiday. The heat weighed so heavily, it seemed as though the sun was trying to press us into the sidewalk.

"That was a pretty sorry excuse for a parade," I said finally by way of an apology. "I'll bet you've seen a whole lot better in Chicago."

But Dorinda still said nothing. Her head drooped forward, like a too-heavy bloom on a slender stem.

"I thought that little GI was kind of cute, though."

Not a word.

"Dorinda? Are you mad at me or something?"

Still no answer.

And that's the way it went all the rest of the way to her boxcar home. She said nothing, answered not a single one of my questions, just walked more and more slowly, her arms hanging from her shoulders as though they had grown loose in their sockets, her head riding lower and lower until I had to double over and peer back toward the sky to see her face.

And that's the way we were still walking, except that I had finally fallen silent, too, when we arrived, at last, in front of the boxcar.

"You want me to stay?" I asked.

Dorinda shook her head.

"Well . . . why don't you give me my red shorts, then? I need to take them home."

"You can get your shorts tomorrow," Dorinda said, her voice flat, lifeless.

I was exasperated and was just about to tell her so—after all, she was the one who had wanted to go to the parade in the first place—when a tall man emerged from around the back of the boxcar. He was wearing work clothes—tan pants and a short-sleeve seersucker shirt, just what my dad wore to work on summer days, and as my father always did, he carried a safety helmet in one hand. His dark hair was cropped close against his head, and his skin glowed the same blue-black as Dorinda's.

"Good Lord!" The man came to an abrupt halt. He closed his eyes as though, when he opened them again, the scene before him would have changed. In the stillness of that pause, his face might have been carved from ebony.

"Dorinda?" he inquired, when his gaze was on her again. "Baby?"

Dorinda didn't answer. She just burst into noisy sobs and threw herself into her father's arms.

He swooped her up and held her against his chest in a tight hug. An almost electric current passed through me. Could it have been jealousy? I couldn't remember my father ever holding me so close . . . not even when I was much younger. After a moment, Dorinda's father looked down at the LIBERTY sign around her neck and then over at my FRIEND OF LIBERTY.

"Where did you take my little girl?" he asked. His voice was low and perfectly controlled, but his glare pinned me to the spot.

Where did I take her? As though I was in charge! Still, I told him the truth. "We've been to the Fourth of July parade."

"Here? In this town?" he asked, incredulous.

"In this town," I admitted. "Dorinda . . . she wanted to go."

"And what happened?" His voice was as dark as his glowering face.

"They . . . They . . ."

"They humiliated her, didn't they?"

My mouth opened, ready to protest, to say, *No! Of course not! The mayor, the city clerk, all the people of my town wouldn't do such a thing to your little girl!* But my mouth shut again of its own accord. I nodded. Yes, they *had* humiliated Dorinda. All of them. Even the "innocent" children.

"I told them she was my cousin . . . visiting from Chicago," I said. "But I don't suppose they believed me."

Mr. Smith's mouth twitched, just one corner, as though a smile might be trying to escape. But he said only, "I think it's time for you to go home."

I nodded again, took a last look at Dorinda, her face still buried in her daddy's neck, and turned away.

What I wanted to say was, "It ain't no home of mine, you know," but, of course, I couldn't.

I couldn't deny it. Osborne belonged to me, and I to the town.

When I arrived at my pleasant, rambling old house, I found my parents waiting for me. Someone had called, more than one someone. Someone who had recognized me with Dorinda. Someone who had overheard the remark about her being my cousin. Someone who was thoroughly shocked that their daughter would do and say such a thing.

Mom and Dad were calm but persistent. Who was she? How had I met her? What had the two of us been doing all this time, hidden away? Why hadn't I told the girl that going to the parade in Osborne wasn't a good idea?

I explained and explained and explained, and they stood there, apparently listening. But when I said, finally, "The mayor was awful. He humiliated her. We should write a letter and complain!" my father let a laugh slip out, a single, sharp bark.

"Who do you want to write a letter to?" he asked.

"I don't know. To the police. To the city council. Maybe to the governor of Illinois. We've got to tell somebody. What he did was wrong!"

My mother said nothing, just turned away to finish shelling the hardboiled eggs she'd prepared for the picnic.

My father shook his head. "Sometimes," he said, looking down on me from the height of weary adult wisdom, "it's better to let sleeping dogs lie."

And then he, too, turned away, through with the discussion.

I stood in the middle of the kitchen, shock racing

through my bones. *Sleeping dogs?* As though that's all my community was, a dog that wouldn't bite if only left to its slumber. Didn't anyone understand?

Who in this entire town would take responsibility for what had happened to Liberty on the Fourth of July?

V

The next morning, soon after the mill whistle blew to signal that the morning shift had begun, I stood in the grass in front of the boxcar, once more cradling a grocery bag of dolls in my arms. Prudy lay on the top, her white dress newly washed and starched and pressed—my mother had helped me—and her pink taffeta coat and hat ironed, too. I had even put a bit of white polish on her shoes. Now that Dorinda's father knew about me, there was no reason for Dorinda not to have the doll she loved.

I called Dorinda's name. It's what we kids did, stood outside a house and called a friend's name rather than going up and knocking on the door. I suppose it was a way of avoiding adults, though it was merely habit, too, as I knew Dorinda would be alone.

For a long moment there was no answer, and I called again. Finally, slowly, the door slid open and Dorinda stood in the shadowy doorway, wearing the bright yellow sundress of our first encounter. She held a book in her hands, and she seemed to be reading it.

"Do you want your shorts?" she asked without looking up.

Do I want my shorts? "Sure," I said, tamping down the irritation that I felt. "But I came to play. Don't you want to play?"

She didn't answer, just dropped the book onto the couch beside her, picked up my carefully folded red shorts, and tossed them to me. I tucked them down inside the grocery bag and shifted my weight. Wasn't she going to invite me in?

She wasn't. What she said, finally, was, "My daddy says I can't play with you anymore."

I hugged the grocery bag closer, blinking back tears. However we had started out, Dorinda hadn't been only someone to occupy my days, someone to appreciate my stories. She had been a friend . . . a good one. I'd always known our time together would have to end with the summer—or whenever before the summer was up that her father took her back to Chicago—but I wasn't ready for all of it to come to an end yet.

"Do you think maybe we could play anyway?" I pleaded. "Even if your daddy says no? You weren't supposed to play with me—or anybody else—before, and you did."

She gazed at her feet and shrugged. "I'd better do what he says this time. Anyhow, we'll be going home soon. He's just about finished his work. And I don't want to get into any more trouble."

I stared at her, at her blue-black skin against the sunny yellow of the dress. The part in her tightly braided hair looked vulnerable somehow.

"Well, then," I said, finally, dipping into the bag to pull

out the big doll. "Even if we can't play anymore, I came to bring you Prudy. Your father knows about me now, so there's no reason you can't have her."

Dorinda came down the steps toward me, her eyes intent on the doll. But she didn't put out her hands to receive her gift. Instead, she stopped in front of me and asked, "You're really going to give her to me?"

"Sure. I told you before you could have her. Besides, if you have Prudy . . . well, then," I hesitated. ". . . I thought maybe you'd remember me."

Would she want to remember me? I gazed into her eyes, seeking an answer.

Her hands remained folded behind her back. "Don't worry," she said. "I'll remember you." It might have been the kind of promise one friend makes to another. But then she added, "I'll remember Osborne, too."

I flinched.

But even as she spoke, Dorinda's hands emerged slowly, reaching for the doll. They might have been moving against her will. She lifted Prudy gently from my grasp, then held her out at arms' length, tipping her back and up again, watching the blue eyes open and close. She drew the doll close, tucking the bonneted head beneath her chin.

"I'll take her," she said, "but only if you let me give you something to remember me by, too."

"Sure!" I answered, eager now. "That would be nice." And I immediately began to try to figure what she might give me. Her Margaret O'Brien paper dolls? She knew I loved Margaret O'Brien.

Dorinda handed Prudy back to me. "Here. You hold her for a minute." She turned and ran up the steps into the boxcar.

I held Prudy close, thinking about the possibilities of the exchange. Dorinda had a set of tempura paints that I loved, too. They were so much better than the plain old watercolors I had at home.

She emerged again, her hands once more behind her back. "Ready?" she asked, her eyes sparkling in that familiar way.

"Ready," I promised.

And she brought from behind her back the brown rubber doll I'd seen that first day and had never thought about since. Instantly I smiled, the kind of smile you slap on your face when someone has made an awkward mistake and you don't want to embarrass her. *A naked rubber baby doll in exchange for my elegant doll with her taffeta coat and her lace-trimmed bonnet? What could Dorinda be thinking?*

"Oh," I said. "Thank you." But even as I said it, even as I reached to make the exchange, my artificial smile melted under a flood of pure, hot shame. For the first time, I realized what I had done.

For weeks Dorinda and I had been playing dolls, in the boxcar, in our special place in the woods, in my room, and I had never once thought to suggest that her doll could be part of our story. The world we had created—that I had created with my stories—was as deeply and completely segregated as the towns of Lafayette-Pearson-Osborne. And I had never even noticed!

Why, I wondered, had Dorinda, as strong as she was, as bossy as she could be, never demanded that her doll be included? Unless she had looked into my heart and seen who I was: a girl who had lived her entire life in a white ghetto. A girl from whom nothing more could be expected.

"Thank you," I said again, folding the brown doll into my arms. And this time I truly meant it.

"Her name's Tabitha," Dorinda said.

I looked down at the chubby brown face. The doll was made from the same mold that Caucasian rubber dolls were made from. I had seen them often. The two were exactly alike, except that this one was a rich chocolate brown, and her eyes were dark and deep.

"Tabitha," I repeated. "I like that."

Dorinda nodded once, then turned away. Reluctantly, I did, too.

"Thank you!" I called back over my shoulder when I reached the edge of the clearing. "Thank you for . . . everything."

But Dorinda had already gone back inside the boxcar. I knew I would never see her again.

I knew, too, that she had no idea just what I was thanking her for.

In a summer of robin's-egg-blue skies, I had, for the very first time, glimpsed the world in color.

New Girl

I stood in front of the seventh-grade class, my gaze lowered so I wouldn't have to see all those faces focused on me like spotlights.

"This is Claire Davis," Mrs. Carson, my new seventh-grade teacher, was saying. I didn't know it then, on that September day in 1950, but for the next two years, until I graduated from this school, the teachers would nearly always add "Davis" to my name when calling on me. My mother was a kindergarten teacher in another school in the same town, and the teachers seemed to need to remind themselves each time they said my name that I was my mother's daughter, a person to treat with respect if not necessarily affection.

Even Mr. Valenzo, the music teacher, the one all the girls were in love with, would address me that way. He'd give nicknames to the other girls—Bubbles, Giggles, Freckles, Red—but when calling on me he'd intone with sudden seriousness, "ClaireDavis," as though the two names were one.

That first morning, though, I didn't notice. I *chose* not to notice. I had spent the summer dreaming of this change, and I was determined not to see any negatives. My mother had suggested the transfer after a spring teachers' strike at my school in Osborne threatened to carry over into the next school year. Though my father was fiercely pro-labor, pro-union, Mom didn't approve of strikes for teachers. Teachers were professionals, she said, and above striking. She also thought the schools in Pearson, the town where she taught, were better than the one I'd been attending in our own town.

At first, I liked the idea of going to a new school. I saw the transfer as a chance to start over. I hadn't exactly been popular at my school in Osborne. I was too "out of it," too much off in my own dreams and oblivious to the world of popular songs and movie stars and boys that increasingly occupied the other girls in my class. But now all that was going to change. I'd spent the whole summer preparing for the change.

I'd listened to the Top Ten all summer, and I knew that this week "Tennessee Waltz," sung by Patti Page, was number one on the charts. I'd even tried to keep track of the actors when I went to the movies. Not ones like The Three Stooges or Abbott and Costello. Nobody cared about them. But the romantic kind—Cary Grant, for instance. The truth was, I didn't like Cary Grant all that much. He was too slick. Or perhaps, he was simply too male. I liked Margaret O'Brien and Yvonne DeCarlo, but neither of them was especially popular with other girls. I liked Margaret O'Brien because she danced, as I did, and Yvonne DeCarlo usually played a woman on a pirate ship and wore a low-cut blouse that revealed her cleavage. It was the low-cut blouse I liked.

I wouldn't talk about those things to anyone, though. I'd figured that out this past summer—not to say things like that. In fact, I'd figured out just about everything I'd ever done wrong in my former school, and this time I was going to do all of it right.

I'd even decided I was going to try out as a cheerleader. Not just try out—I intended to make the squad. Maybe I would even be the cheerleading captain. After all, I'd studied ballet and tap and acrobatics since I was four years old. I could jump and arch my back and flip my little pleated skirt with the best of them! I knew I could.

But now, I stood before the class, my hands too clumsy and too large, my head looming above my body like a jack-o'-lantern. I might even have been grinning like a jack-o'-lantern. I felt so disconnected from myself that I couldn't tell.

I looked down at my bright new saddle shoes and my thin blue anklets that matched the blue in my dress. I'd chosen the saddle shoes, but my mother had picked out the colored anklets. Mom thought the thick white bobby socks the other girls wore were ugly. I had always agreed with her, though now, standing in front of my new class, I wondered: Were bobby socks something I should have thought about and hadn't? Maybe my mother was wrong about socks. Maybe she was wrong about changing schools, too.

"Why are you here?" the roomful of stares demanded to know. "You don't belong," they said.

Mrs. Carson directed me to a seat on the left-hand side, toward the front of the room. I sat down across from a girl with blunt-cut brown hair pulled back on one side with a barrette. She wore a homemade dress with green stripes and too-long, too-narrow, too-ugly brown oxfords. And thin green anklets.

"Hi," the girl whispered. "My name is Pauline."

"Hi," I whispered back, though I didn't try to sound too friendly. I understood the territory I was in. One look at the girl's hunched shoulders told me all I needed to know. In my last school, I'd been the outsider. Here, that place was already taken by Pauline.

When the noon bell rang, I was relieved to see Pauline leave to walk home for lunch. I could have walked to the primary school where Mother taught and eaten lunch in the faculty lounge, but I'd figured spending lunchtime here at school would give me a good chance to begin making friends. So, waving good-bye to Pauline, a good-bye that wasn't too conspicuous or too enthusiastic, I went to my locker for my sack lunch.

When I returned to the classroom with my brown bag, it took almost more courage than I possessed to walk the length of the room to the back corner by the windows where the other girls who didn't go home for lunch were gathered.

"Hi," I said when I finally arrived and stood hesitating by an empty desk.

The girls were leaning toward one another, talking.

"Hi," one of them said in a flat, unwelcoming voice, and they returned to their conversation.

I sat down and unrolled the top of my lunch bag, heat crawling up my neck.

The talk ricocheted from topic to topic, but it was mostly about people—people I'd never heard of. None of my research from the summer seemed to apply. I chewed my sandwich, not even noticing what kind it was, and listened, waiting for a chance to jump in.

When a girl I'd heard referred to as Donna said something about dance class, I came to attention. Dance class! That was something I could talk about. I spent every Saturday at Mrs. Madison's dance studio and even assisted sometimes with teaching the younger classes, demonstrating the exercises while Mrs. Madison moved up and down the line, correcting technique.

"Oh," I said, my voice high and artificially cheerful. "Do you take dance lessons?"

Donna turned toward me for the first time. "Sure," she said. Nothing more.

Still, it was an opening, and I seized it. "I take dance," I told them. "Ballet and tap and acrobatics. But it's ballet I really love. At Grace Madison's Studio in Lafayette."

They were all looking at me, but no one said anything, so I kept going. There seemed to be nothing to do but to keep going. "Mrs. Madison is a really good teacher. She used to be a ballerina, you know, with . . . well, I don't remember the name of the company she was with, but it was one of the major ones. She's the best dance teacher in town. The only one who's any good . . . really."

I stumbled to a stop, my mouth suddenly dry. Everyone was silent.

"I take lessons from Mrs. Boyd," Donna said finally, and she turned back to her friends.

How could I have been so stupid? I knew about Mrs. Boyd. She was the *other* dance teacher in town. Since I didn't know this girl, it should have been obvious to me that she studied with Mrs. Boyd. I folded the top of my brown paper bag down over the rest of my lunch and carried it back to my locker.

Maybe tomorrow I would eat lunch at my mother's school. Maybe I would even check out which way Pauline walked home. If we happened to be going in the same direction, perhaps we could walk together.

Pauline did walk in the same direction as I. In fact, I found out that she lived only about a block and a half from the school where my mother taught, so we fell into step with one another at the end of the day.

"What do you do after school?" she asked, and she seemed genuinely interested to know.

"Well . . ." I scrambled for the right answer. I couldn't tell her that I often played with dolls, making up stories for them to act out. I took a careful sideways look at her, at her warm brown eyes beneath the home-cut hair. (My mother occasionally cut my hair, too, so I recognized the signs.) "Sometimes I like to make up stories," I said, giving her the safe half of the answer.

"Neat," she said. Then after a moment she added, "Maybe you'll be a writer some day."

It was my solemn dream to be a writer, but it was a dream I'd never shared with anyone—not my teachers, not the girls I used to make up stories for in the neighborhood, certainly not my family. I could only nod, my whole body warming with pleasure and a sudden gratitude for the way Pauline had seen into my heart.

"What do you do?" I asked. "After school, I mean."

She shrugged. "Mostly I take care of my baby brother."

"You have a baby brother?!" I took a deep breath. "How wonderful!"

Pauline wrinkled her nose. "Not exactly. All he does is get into my stuff and wet his diapers. And you ought to try changing a dirty one sometime! You have to dip it in the toilet to get the poop off before you can put it in the diaper pail. It's really gross."

Instantly, on the authority of my new friend, I revised my idea about the wonders of baby brothers.

We walked in a comfortable silence for a few moments, and then she said, her voice low as though conveying an important secret, "The girls at school are kind of stuck up, aren't they?" Before I had a chance to agree, she rushed on. "I don't care, of course. I've got lots of friends at church."

I nodded, believing her. "I've got friends at dance school," I said. I realized as I said it that it was true, so I said it again. "I take lessons at Grace Madison's Dance School every Saturday, and I've got lots of friends there. And the girls in this school *are* stuck up."

Pauline laughed. She threw her head back and tossed her laughter high. She even skipped for a few steps before she twirled around to face me. "Who do you think is the biggest snob of the bunch?" she asked.

I thought about it. I didn't really know them yet. One seemed no worse—or no better—than another. But then I remembered the girl who took dance lessons.

"You know the one with the curly red hair? I think her name is Donna?"

Pauline nodded. "Yeah. Donna Brumbaugh."

"Well, she thinks she's so great because she takes dance lessons from Mrs. Boyd, and Mrs. Boyd doesn't know anything. If you go to one of her recitals, in every single dance, no matter what kind it's supposed to be, everybody does *the step.*"

"What's *the step?*" Pauline asked.

Instead of trying to explain, I took hold of one foot, held it up and hopped in a clumsy circle, showing her *the step.* I'd once heard Mrs. Madison say Mrs. Boyd stuck it in the middle of every dance because she was too unimaginative to think of anything better.

Pauline laughed and laughed. I had to love her.

The next morning, I had no choice but to arrive early since my mother needed to be at her own school well before the opening bell. I stood alone, off to one side, searching the playground for Pauline. She wasn't among the tight clusters of girls that formed here and there, and she wasn't standing off by herself, either. Apparently, she made sure not to get to school early, something I would have been glad to avoid doing, too.

When the bell finally rang, allowing us entrance to the building, Pauline still hadn't arrived. I went to my locker and stood staring into it while the other students rumbled all around me, calling to one another, dropping books, slamming locker doors.

Gathering the books from my locker took all of thirty seconds. Another bell wouldn't send us to our classrooms for ten long minutes.

I decided to go in anyway. I could check my math problems to make sure they were all right, or maybe just look at the pictures in my geography book. I'd already found a picture of a rain forest in there that looked like a leafy cave, a cave where I would have gladly curled up and stayed. But when I reached the door of the classroom and looked in, something warned me. I couldn't have said what it was. Maybe it was the instinct I'd been trying to develop over the summer, the one for self-preservation. There were three—no, four—boys in the room, and Mrs. Carson. She was in the back of the room, putting something up on the bulletin board. But no girls. Not a single one.

I hovered in the open doorway, trying to decide what to do. Why not go in? No reason—right? It was my classroom . . . mine as much as any other student's there.

But when I glanced over my shoulder, I saw two girls standing a short distance away, staring at me like owls watching a hapless mouse.

"Look," one of them said, not even bothering to lower her voice. "She's going to go in."

"With all those boys," the other one added.

And then I understood. I had come close to breaking an unspoken rule in this school. Clearly, no girl could enter the classroom until she had other girls to go in with her. Only *that kind* of girl walked alone into a room already occupied by boys.

I was definitely not *that kind* of girl.

I turned away, dodging my near-fatal mistake, and headed for the girls' lavatory instead. Surely it was safe to go in there.

But when I pushed through the heavy swinging doors, I found half a dozen girls from my class gathered in front of the mottled mirrors, combing their hair, applying bright lipstick—my mother didn't allow lipstick, of course—and chittering like early-morning birds. At least, that's what they were doing until they caught a glimpse of me. Then all talk stopped. The silence couldn't have been more complete if I'd gone instantly deaf.

I stared at the mirrored eyes staring back at me, then turned around and pushed out to the hall again. Laughter trailed after me like poison gas.

I returned to stand in front of my locker, rearranging my books. When Pauline finally arrived, I greeted her like the long-lost friend she had already come to be.

The days settled into a routine. The early mornings never grew easier, but there was always the respite of the walks to and from lunch and then back to my mother's school again in the afternoon with Pauline. As day followed day, our talk grew more intimate. Once we even admitted the unthinkable to one another . . . that neither of us had the slightest desire to grow up.

"Grownups never have any fun," I said.

"All they ever do is work," Pauline agreed.

What we didn't talk about, beyond our initial acknowledgment that the other girls were "stuck up," was being outsiders. And I never once admitted the big plans I'd once had for the new school.

When it came time for cheerleading tryouts, I didn't go. I knew better.

If you are the problem, I told myself solemnly, *then moving to a new place doesn't help. You just take yourself with you.* But I didn't say that to Pauline, either.

And I completely forgot my initial reluctance to align myself with an outsider.

It turned out that the church where Pauline had friends was the Baptist one, and very strict. She wasn't allowed to dance. She wasn't allowed to go to movies, either. What she *was* allowed to do, besides baby-sit her brother, was attend the Bible study class her stepmother held at their house every Thursday after school. (Pauline's mother had died when Pauline was very small, and her father had remarried a woman from their church just a couple of years before, hence the baby brother. And though Pauline didn't say much beyond the complaint about having to baby-sit, everyone knew about wicked stepmothers.)

I wasn't especially interested in studying the Bible, but

I joined the class anyway. At least on that one day, it gave Pauline and me more time together and occupied me until my mother was ready to go home.

The class itself turned out to be painless enough, not much different from going to Sunday school at St. Mark's, the Episcopal church I attended. Pauline's stepmother, Mrs. Tillman, told Bible stories with the aid of flat cutouts that adhered to a flannel board, mostly men in bathrobes accompanied by an occasional woman or camel or flock of sheep. I could always tell which one of the bathrobed men was supposed to be Jesus, because his hair was shaped into a long brown pageboy, and he had cocker-spaniel eyes. I could tell, too, because Mrs. Tillman's voice took on a deeper, more "meaningful" resonance whenever she was moving Jesus around on the board.

I didn't say much about the Bible classes at home. My dad had no use for church, and Hugh usually opted out of services, too. And while Mother belonged to the Episcopal Church, she usually sent me with friends rather than attending herself. In any case, the Bible class wasn't a topic I was inclined to bring up with my family.

School itself continued to be painful; the mornings diddling in front of my locker, excruciating; classes such as gym, where teams were chosen up, agonizing. The academics weren't bad. I was a pretty good student, though I sometimes dreamed my time away and ended up scrambling to get my homework done. That my dreams might prove to be productive someday never occurred to anyone . . . least of all me.

One Thursday, Bible class day, my mother had a teachers' meeting over the noon hour, so I stayed at school to eat my lunch. This time, though, I sat down at my own desk with my brown bag instead of going back to the girls gathered in their distant corner.

"Oh, Claire," Mrs. Carson called cheerfully from her desk where she was eating her own lunch. "Why don't you go join the other girls? Don't sit there by yourself!"

I smiled politely and took out my waxed-paper-wrapped sandwich. There were some things adults seemed unable to comprehend. Maybe the world had been different when Mrs. Carson was young. Maybe girls had been different then, too.

When I didn't move, she left me alone to concentrate on my sandwich and rapidly warming milk, but after a while she seemed compelled to pay attention to me again.

"How is your mother?" she asked. Her voice resonated in the mostly empty room, and behind me, the chatter of the girls in the lunch corner fell silent.

"Fine," I replied, ducking my head and scrabbling in my lunch bag to see what else was in there.

"Does she have a lot of kindergartners this year?"

I couldn't remember. Mom had probably talked about how many students she had, but I hadn't been paying attention. "I guess so," I mumbled.

But Mrs. Carson wasn't about to be put off by an unenthusiastic response. She just shifted topic. "That was a fine essay you wrote on rain forests," she said. "It's one of the best papers I've seen from a seventh-grader."

One of the best papers! I was thrilled . . . and I couldn't help but be glad that the girls in back had heard. Had Mrs. Carson ever said such a thing to one of them?

I found myself responding as if Mrs. Carson had hit my talk button. I told her all the things I'd learned about the rain forest that hadn't made their way into my paper. I told her about a Tarzan movie I'd seen and how inaccurate the film's depiction of a tropical rain forest—or jungle, as they called it—had been. I even told her how much I liked to write. And when the other girls left for the playground, I folded my empty lunch sack and trailed out after them, feeling wondrously full.

But when I emerged into the hall, I found three of the girls huddled together outside the door. As I passed, a name grabbed at me like a hand reaching out and taking hold of the back of my neck. "Brownnose!"

The name choked the breath out of me, and I almost came to a full stop right there, right next to them. I caught myself, though, and hurried on, tears trembling behind my eyelids. Was there *nothing* I could do right in this school?

Pauline would be back from lunch soon. She would know how unfair the remark had been.

When Pauline finally did arrive, though, she was full of talk of her baby brother—the milk he had spilled, the peas he had tossed from his highchair, the way her stepmother cooed over him no matter how horrible he was being. I listened in a mechanical way, nodding my head. I started to tell her what had happened, but I found my mouth wouldn't form the words. Brownnose. No one had ever called me a brownnose in my former school.

When school was out that day, I walked with Pauline to her house for the Bible study class, my feet leaden. Everything was too hard. Staying in this school. Going back to my old one. Attending Mrs. Tillman's Bible class. Making excuses for not going. I had developed the first signs of a cold during the endless afternoon and could have used that as my excuse for skipping the class, but even saying the words seemed to require more effort than I could muster.

I followed Pauline through her back door and across the kitchen and settled into the semicircle of chairs in the dining room with the few other girls, none in our class at school, who attended the Bible study. A fragrant pot roast bubbled on the stove in the kitchen, and Pauline's baby brother, the highchair spiller and tosser, babbled happily in a playpen in a corner of the dining room. I sighed deeply and pulled my cardigan more snugly around my shoulders. At least no one would call me a brownnose here.

This Thursday, Mrs. Tillman seemed more excited than usual, but she began the class routinely enough, telling a story of one of Jesus' many healings as she moved the paper-doll figures around on the flannel board. The story flowed past me like a gentle breeze. Something to be enjoyed without particularly noticing that it was there— certainly without stopping to wonder what it might mean.

I blew my nose, wriggled a bit in the squeaky folding chair, peeked at the baby. Even if his poopy diapers were disgusting, he was awfully cute.

Then Mrs. Tillman made a shift she'd never made before. Her voice shifted, too, coming from some more resonant, more deeply felt place.

"Do you need a friend?" she asked. "I know I do."

Why does she need a friend? I wondered. Pauline's stepmother had a husband, a baby . . . even Pauline. Grownups didn't need friends, did they?

"Jesus will be your friend," she continued, and I thought, *Oh . . . that.* I'd heard it before. Who hadn't?

"He loves you," Mrs. Tillman was saying. "Even when no one else does. Jesus is knocking on the door to your heart, and only you can open your heart and let Him in."

Open your heart and let Him in. That wasn't the way Episcopalians talked. We learned about Jesus in Sunday school, of course, but more the way we learned about George Washington and Abraham Lincoln in school—a history lesson dressed up in miracles.

"Jesus is knocking on the door to your heart right now," Mrs. Tillman repeated. "But there is something unusual about that door. The handle is on the inside, so He can't open it and walk in. He has to wait for you to open it for Him."

I didn't know whether Episcopalians were expected to open their hearts for Jesus or not. But if we were, I was certain we were supposed to open that door very quietly, completely privately, without making any kind of fuss.

"Jesus will be your friend," Pauline's stepmother said. "Jesus will never leave you. No matter how sad you are or how lost, no matter how difficult your life may seem, if you invite Him into your heart, He'll be your friend forever."

Forever. The word passed through me, through my gut—or maybe it was my heart—neatly and quickly, like the sharpest of blades. *My friend forever!*

A chill started at my scalp and vibrated through my entire body, right down to the soles of my feet. I must have shivered, because Pauline turned to look at me, eyebrows lifted.

And then Mrs. Tillman was inviting us to "Come forward and give yourselves to the Lord." She looked right at me as she said it, right inside me.

And in that instant, the image of a friend waiting forever for me to open the door to my heart overwhelmed me. What would it be like to have Jesus beside me when I waited in front of my locker every morning? Could He make comments like "brownnose" go away? Maybe He understood about nasty girls. Maybe He even knew what to do about them!

I readjusted my cardigan around my shoulders and tried to push the image away, but something of the chill that had passed through me must have shown in my face. Mrs. Tillman stepped toward me, asking earnestly, "Claire? Are you all right?"

Pauline was watching me, too. I could feel her gaze like an insistent question pressing into my flesh.

I nodded abruptly, dismissing them both, but my feet seemed to have another idea. They planted themselves on the floor, stood me up, and carried me right into Mrs. Tillman's waiting arms.

My feet had decided, without consulting my head, that I would be "saved." And there I stood, in front of Pauline and the other girls, weeping joyous tears!

At least, when I felt their warmth on my cheeks, I told myself that they must be tears of joy.

At dinner that evening, my astonishing experience still glowed in my belly. I looked at my small family, the four of us, gathered around the yellow Formica table, and I loved them all with an ardor I had never felt before. That was because I now loved them with the love of Jesus, something I knew my poor blind family had no knowledge of at all.

My mother was too closed down to feelings, my brother too arrogant, my father too cynical. I watched them all covertly from beneath my eyebrows as they applied themselves to their food. My father vigorously shook salt and then pepper onto everything on his plate. (My mother was a very bland cook.) He, I knew, was especially impervious to religion. Was it his fierce intelligence that made him so skeptical? How could anyone ever explain to a chemist that some things couldn't be understood with the mind? Like the love of Jesus!

I pitied them all. My newfound joy, my certainty that I had—at last—found the way, filled me. And I wanted . . . oh, how desperately I wanted to share the gift I had been given with these three people I loved.

I knew better. With every fiber of my being, I knew that I could never tell my family what had happened to me that day. But it seemed impossible to keep it to myself. No wonder the Bible was called *The Good News*! It told us that we had a friend forever. And what could be better news than that?

"I accepted Jesus today," I blurted, and even as I spoke, I thrust my chin out, ready to take them all on.

My mother looked up from the pork chop she was cutting and frowned.

Hugh let out a sudden, sharp snort, an expression of amusement and disdain.

My father, the scientist, the man who often found his daughter inane, put his fork down and smiled at me. The smile was holding back amusement in a way that gave instant warning.

"And what did you accept about Jesus?" he asked. The question dripped innocence.

He knew. I was certain he knew *exactly* what I was talking about. He had grown up in an evangelical church and still loved to listen to gospel music on the radio, even though he never attended services of any stripe.

"I mean," I said, already realizing I was cornered, "I took Jesus into my heart. I was saved."

"From?"

I stared at my father blankly.

He clarified his question. "Saved from what?"

"From sin," I said. "Of course." Before that moment, the word "sin" had probably never been spoken in our

65

cheerful kitchen. It came out sounding too loud and somehow in poor taste.

Dad's smile never wavered. He was enjoying himself. "And there was a lot of sin in your life to be saved from, was there?"

"Enough," I answered, the first licks of anger already anticipating my defeat. It was the way I lost most arguments with my father, by letting him push me into anger. "Everybody sins, you know."

"Do you want to tell us about your sins?" Hugh asked, leering at me cheerfully from the other end of the Formica table.

"It's not just about sin," I snapped. It was easier to snap at Hugh than at my father. "Accepting Jesus is about having a friend . . . forever." For some reason I couldn't have explained, my eyes had started to sting.

"Claire." Mother laid a hand over one of mine. "It's not—"

I pulled my hand away, and she didn't finish whatever she had started to say.

"A friend who's been dead for two thousand years," my father said in that same "agreeable" voice. "Sounds like fun."

"But He's not dead! He still lives. That's the whole point!"

This time my father said nothing, but he exchanged a look with my mother that said, as clearly as anything he could have spoken, *Here we go with more of Claire's foolishness!*

66

I was on my feet for the second time that day. "It's always the same," I cried, addressing myself to my father. "You don't believe in anything . . . nothing you can't weigh or measure or count. When I come home with a husband someday, you'll probably tell me you don't even believe in love."

"No," Dad replied, his smile broad and uncomplicated, genuine at last. "The day you come home with a husband, that's when I'll start believing in miracles!"

It was a familiar theme. Because I was . . . well, all the things I was—irrational, illogical, emotional, too easily driven to anger and to the tears with which my anger was usually expressed—my father assumed that no one, certainly no man, would ever want me.

I ran upstairs to my room and slammed the door and, of course, proved my father entirely right by throwing myself on the bed, sobbing.

I should have known better. I *did* know better. Why hadn't I kept my mouth shut?

And why hadn't this Jesus I'd just given my heart to saved me from making such a dumb mistake?

But lying on my bed, feeling the pillow beneath my cheek grow damp, I wasn't sure which mistake I most wanted Him to have saved me from. The mistake of confessing my new faith to my unbelieving family? Or the one of being so foolish, so much the irrational, emotional girl my father knew me to be, as to stand up and be "saved"?

Now, enveloped in the familiar quiet of my room, I

cringed at the memory of the commotion that had followed my simple rising from my chair. The promises of
heaven, the extravagant rejoicing. Mrs. Tillman's arms
around me; I'd never liked Mrs. Tillman all that much.
The way Pauline had said to me afterward, "Now you're
one of us." As though we hadn't really been friends before
that moment.

What had I done? How could I have been so foolish?
Whatever these people dreamed, it was not my dream. I
knew that. I must have known that, even in the first
moment I rose from my chair. But Mrs. Tillman had dan-
gled a lure in front of me, and I'd leapt like any hungry
fish.

A friend forever! What a notion. What an incredible bit
of whimsy to carry a person through a difficult day.

The truth was, I knew that however wide I flung open
the door to my heart, Jesus would never be *my* friend. No
matter that I occupied a pew in church most Sundays; I
had been inoculated with my father's deep cynicism. I
was immune to God.

The next morning, Pauline arrived at school early and
sought me out on the playground, her face aglow. "Aren't
you happy?" she asked, wrapping her arms around me in
an extravagant hug, something she had never done
before.

How could I tell her? Was it possible to change your
mind about being saved? How did you get un-saved once
you'd stood up in a Bible study class?

"I was so excited last night," she continued, gliding right over my lack of response. "So excited for you, I could hardly sleep. Oh, Claire, you're one of the saints now. Isn't that wonderful?"

One of the saints. I was one of the saints. I almost wanted to laugh.

I took a step backward, extricating myself from Pauline's embrace. "Uh . . . Pauline," I said. "There's something I've got to tell you."

She knew. I could tell instantly that she knew what I was going to say, and the lively joy drained from her face in a rush. She didn't say anything, though; she just stood there, her arms limp against the sides of that same ugly green dress she'd been wearing the first time I'd seen her. Her stepmother must have made the dress for her. Mrs. Tillman was a pretty woman—petite and pretty. She dressed nicely, too. Maybe she *wanted* Pauline to be ugly . . . sort of like the stepmother in *Snow White*.

"I've . . . ," I stumbled. "I mean . . . well . . ."

Pauline said nothing, did nothing to help, just waited.

"I wanted to tell you. And I thought maybe you could tell your stepmother for me. I—I thought about it after, and I've decided it was all a mistake."

"A mistake?" Pauline's voice rose above the general hubbub of a group of fourth graders running past, playing tag. "A mistake?" she repeated, and her voice increased in volume. "You can't make a mistake about being saved. It's not possible!"

"Shh!" I struggled with the urge to put a hand up to

cover her mouth. All I needed was to have the other girls hear. This was a strongly Roman Catholic community. Most of our classmates gained entrance to heaven by the right combination of prayers recited and sins confessed. Which meant I knew exactly what they would think about my being "saved." They would think that I was odd for Jesus, like Pauline, on top of being a teacher's brat and a brownnose. It was hard to imagine anything I wanted less.

"It's just . . . it's just," I stumbled on. "I wasn't feeling very good yesterday. This cold, you know?" I took a tattered tissue from my pocket and blew my nose to prove my point. "And I'd heard somebody saying something kind of bad . . . about me. So I was . . . I guess I was just kind of . . ." I struggled for the word and couldn't find it.

"I know what you were 'just.'" Pauline's voice was low now. Low and exceedingly angry. "You were just making fun of us, weren't you? That's what you were doing."

"No!" I cried. "No, it wasn't like that at all!"

But she had already turned away, tossing her final words over her shoulder. "Do you know what happens to people like you, Claire Davis?" She didn't wait to find out if I knew. She went right on to tell me. "They go to hell. That's what happens. They burn in hell forever!"

Several of the girls stopped their conversation to look at us—to stare, really.

I turned away, wishing the bell would ring. If the bell would only ring, I could go stand in front of my locker.

At least, I consoled myself, I didn't have to worry about

the threat of hellfire, whatever Pauline said. My father's skeptical mind had made me immune to that, too . . . or at least to the fear of it.

That afternoon, the seventh-grade girls gathered in the seats at the edge of the gym, waiting for our teacher to appear. Pauline and I sat off to one side, as usual, but this time several seats away from each other, the two of us looking off in different directions as though the other didn't exist. At noon, we had also managed to walk the same route to lunch and back without coming near each other.

"Pauline!"

I looked up to see who was calling. A girl beckoned to Pauline from the clump on the other side. It was Judy, one of the really popular girls.

"Come here," Judy commanded. "We've got something we want to ask you."

Pauline cast a look in my direction. Did she expect some kind of reaction? Maybe a shrug? Or a lifted eyebrow that would say, "Don't go! They can't order you around"?

I gave no signal, just picked studiously at a hangnail and refused to look up again. Obviously, the girls knew we'd had an argument and that this was a time they could slip between us easily. No matter. Let Pauline make up her own mind. The way I'd made up my own mind about Jesus.

Pauline stood tentatively, then carried herself over to

the group as though she were delivering a fragile vessel that might too easily be broken or spilled. She sat down in an empty seat on the fringe of the group.

"We were just wondering," Judy said, leaning toward her in a friendly way. "I mean, we know you can't take dance lessons or anything like that because of your church, but if you could . . . would you take lessons from Mrs. Madison or from Mrs. Boyd?"

She spoke loudly enough to make sure I could hear the question, too.

Pauline glanced toward me again. She looked panicked, cornered. But before she could see me—really see me—she turned her gaze away again.

"Why, Mrs. Boyd, of course," she answered. And she, too, spoke loudly and distinctly enough for every word to reach my ears. "I think Mrs. Madison's dance school is really dumb."

"Yeah, Pauline!" The girls applauded, and Pauline melted back into the seat, her cheeks bright with pleasure.

Or was it shame? Surely this wasn't the way a saint was supposed to behave.

At the end of the day, I dawdled on the walk to my mother's school. After the last bell rang, Pauline had hung back, pretending to be absorbed in straightening her desk. I'd left without her, but then slowed my pace. We always walked the same route, so I knew she would have to catch up with me sooner or later.

I hadn't gone very far when I heard footsteps approaching tentatively from behind. It was Pauline; it had to be. The steps trailed me for half a block, and I kept moving more and more slowly, first stopping to retie my shoe, then to examine a dandelion growing up through a crack in the walk. Finally, Pauline had no choice but to come alongside.

We walked in silence for a few moments before I reached for my weapon. "Once you're saved," I said, keeping my voice light, as though I were asking a perfectly ordinary question, "what happens when you sin? Do you have to be born again all over?"

She knew immediately what I was referring to. "It wasn't a sin," she said, emphatic and low.

"Wasn't it?" I asked with the same heavily weighted innocence my father so often used against me. And then I added, still in my father's voice, "I thought Jesus was faithful to His friends."

Pauline didn't reply. I looked over at her and could see that her face was red. This time I was certain that what she was feeling was shame, and I was glad.

Finally, she spoke. "I had to choose Mrs. Boyd," she said. "Because of the . . ." But I couldn't hear the rest.

"Because of the *what?*" I asked sharply, increasing my pace. Maybe I didn't want her walking with me, after all.

"Because of the step," she said, quite loudly this time.

"'The step'?" At first I had no idea what she was talking about. But then I remembered. She was talking about the silly step I had once told her about, the one that

73

Mrs. Boyd put in the middle of every dance in her recitals.

I stopped walking, turning to face Pauline, and she stopped, too. She had little choice since I stood directly in her path. "You mean you'd want to take lessons from Mrs. Boyd so you could learn *the step?*"

She nodded, but the barest traces of a smile tickled the corners of her mouth, giving her away.

"This one?" I persisted. And I picked up one foot, held it out in the air, and hopped around in a circle.

"Yeah," she said. "I want to learn to do that. It's so . . ."

But she never finished what she was going to say. She just giggled, and even I couldn't help but smile.

We walked on. "If it had been you they'd called," she said at last, "I'll bet you'd have gone over, too." There was no accusation in her voice. She seemed merely to be stating a fact. She might have said, "If you'd gone out in the rain, you would have gotten wet, too."

Never! I wanted to say. I wanted to cry it so loudly that every girl in the seventh grade heard. But something wouldn't let me. *Maybe she's right,* I found myself thinking. *Maybe I* would *have gone over.* Even though I'd have known—exactly the way I was certain Pauline had known—that the favor I'd earn through my betrayal would be good for about two minutes.

So I offered no argument, just walked along at my friend's side for another block or two. We were getting close to the corner where Pauline turned off when the question came to me, burning to be asked. A real question this time. I stopped to face her once more. "What's it like," I asked, "inviting Jesus into your heart? *Really* doing it, I mean."

She looked away, and at first I thought she wasn't going to answer.

"It's . . . ," she said at last, but she stopped.

I leaned toward her, and she tried again.

"It makes it good," she said.

"Makes what good?" I asked, my breath caught in my chest, waiting to be released.

"Everything," she said finally with a shrug that emphasized the inadequacy of the word, of all words. "Being alive." And though her answer was utterly simple, unembellished, her face glowed with that profound joy I'd seen before when she spoke of Jesus.

The breath I had been holding escaped in a sigh. I believed her. I didn't want to, but I believed her.

We turned and walked on again, by mutual consent stopping at the corner where we had to part. I elbowed her lightly in the ribs. "Do you really want to learn *the step?*" I asked.

A grin spread across her face. "I do," she said.

"Well," I said, "first you pick up your foot like this." And I lifted one foot into my hand, my skirt hiking up above my knees to allow the stretch. "And then . . ."

Pauline lifted her own foot and, laughing, immediately lost her balance and sat down hard in the middle of the sidewalk.

I reached down to help her up. "Are you okay?"

"Yeah," she answered, still laughing. "I'm fine."

When she was on her feet again, though, the laughter trailed off. She stood in front of me, brushing off her ugly green dress and gazing at me intently. "Are *you* okay?" she asked. And I could tell that she really wanted to know.

I hesitated before I answered, long enough to check myself over mentally, as though I had been the one who had just picked myself up from the hard sidewalk. "Yeah," I said, finally. "I'm fine, too."

And I meant it.

Then, giggling wildly, we each picked up a foot in one hand, poked it out into the air, and hopped around in two separate but equally clumsy circles.

Killing Miss Kitty

There was nothing appealing about the dark gray kitten. She was scraggly and flea-bitten and skinny. You
could count her ribs through her fur. She had come into
a world where no one wanted her and been abandoned
before she was old enough to care for herself.

My brother and I were walking near the baseball field
when we found her. The field was a rough one Hugh and
his friends had carved out in the long grass between the
woods and Lexington Avenue, with its double row of
cement mill company houses. The kitten was teetering
on top of the field's homemade backstop, surrounded by
cheering boys.

The boys were taking bets on how high they could
count before the mite lost her frantic hold on the boards
and tumbled to the ground again. Tommy, Fred, Jack—
they were all there. Even Bobby, though he was three
years younger than the rest and wasn't usually tolerated
by them. They were all laughing and slapping each other
on the back . . . and counting.

Putting the scraggly kitten up there on top of the backstop had been Bobby's idea. Maybe that was why the other boys were allowing him to hang around, because he'd come up with such a good idea. Jack was the one who had the bets going.

Hugh and I stood for a few seconds, taking everything in. The excited boys, elbowing one another, egging one another on. The terrified kitten, scrabbling on her perch, needle-like claws extended, tail puffed like a bottle brush, pink mouth open in silent pleading.

It was the last that affected me most, the way she kept opening her mouth without making a sound. The mews seemed to have been frightened right out of her.

I wanted to protest, but I was afraid of the boys. There was a roughness about them that had always intimidated me. So though I longed to rush in and snatch the kitten away, I looked to my older brother instead, hoping he would come to the rescue.

I had never seen the kitten before. She didn't belong to anyone we knew, and from the looks of her no one cared what happened to her. Except for me and, I hoped, Hugh. The kitten didn't look as though she was going to survive much longer if someone didn't interfere with the game she was caught in.

"Hey!" Hugh said to the boys.

The kitten fell again, her legs splayed, her tiny puff of a tail poked straight out behind as if she were trying to turn herself into a parachute. But if that was what she intended, she wasn't very successful. Not only did she fall fast, she didn't even land on her feet. She hit the ground on her side with a soft but perceptible *thud*. It was hard to believe anything so small could make that much of a sound on impact. Harder still to believe she had enough life left in her to claw and bite when Bobby picked her up to return her to the top of the backstop.

"Ow!" Bobby yelled, followed by several stronger words. And he flung his hand, sending the kitten sailing once more. This time she managed to get her feet under her before she landed, though she had less time to prepare.

"Hey!" I said it this time. "You leave that kitten alone!"

The boys turned to gawk at me before they laughed.

But Hugh stepped forward. "I'll take her," he said. "Give the kitten to me."

They weren't keen on stopping their fun, but my brother had a quiet authority, and they gave her to him without too much complaint. I wanted to be the one to carry her home, but Hugh just shook his head and kept her cupped against his chest.

"She'll scratch you," he said. "She doesn't even know how to retract her claws."

Maybe, I thought, *she knows, but she's never felt safe enough to put her weapons away.*

I loved cats. We had one at home named Sooty. We had Sooty despite the fact that our mother had grown up on a farm and didn't really believe in having animals in the house. They belonged, she said, outside or in a barn. But she allowed a cat, partly because I begged for one and partly because it kept down the population of mice that scurried through the walls of our old frame house. When one cat met with some accident, as it inevitably did, we always got another. Sooner or later, someone we knew would be giving away kittens.

Sooty was a tortoiseshell, black with ginger and cream splotches. I was the one who'd named her. I always named the cats, though Hugh sometimes complained about the names I picked. Our favorite cat of all I had called Wee One, a name he'd positively hated. When she went out into the woods one night and didn't return, she'd been replaced by Sooty. Hugh didn't seem to mind the name Sooty.

He liked cats well enough, but he had no use for dogs. He never said, straight out, that he was afraid of dogs, but I'd gone with him on his afternoon paper route a time or two. There were a couple of mutts on the route that came running out, growling and yapping at him, and you needed only to see his face to know that he was scared spitless. I had to admire him, though—he wouldn't give up that route.

Still, my brother was reasonably fond of cats. Sometimes at night he even let Sooty come into his bedroom to sleep on his bed, right behind his knees. That annoyed me. "She's *my* cat," I would tell him, though no one had ever said the cat was mine. "You'd better explain that to Sooty," he always replied.

This kitten, though, would be mine for sure. Entirely.

We found our mother in the kitchen, making strawberry preserves. The steam from the bubbling pot of strawberries filled the kitchen with fragrant heat.

Of course, she said no. We both knew that was what she would say. I took over at that point, arguing, wheedling, describing the horrible death awaiting the poor little thing if we didn't make a home for her.

Hugh went back outside and left the kitten's fate to me. I guess he knew I'd wear Mom down. And, finally, she did give in. Rather, she didn't so much give in as quit arguing. Our dad would argue endlessly on just about any topic at all, so long as you kept up your end of the discussion and didn't use any dirty tricks like tears. I usually lost arguments with Dad for descending into tears. It didn't take much, though, for our mother to run out of arguments . . . and words. Once she did, the kitten settled in.

Hugh named this one. He said since he'd rescued her, she was his to name, and the name he came up with was about what I would have expected from him. He called her Kitty.

I objected. Who wouldn't? Hugh refused to budge, though, so I put my stamp on his choice. I called the indignant puff of gray fur Miss Kitty. Hugh just shrugged and ignored the "Miss" part of her name. And after a while, as usually happened, Miss Kitty ended up belonging to me anyway . . . as much as she could be said to belong to anybody.

Under either name, the tabby kitten did not grow up well. Either because of her rough beginnings at the backstop or earlier deprivations we knew nothing about, she grew into a cranky, disagreeable cat. She would as soon claw you as look at you. And the fierce light in her yellow eyes made her feelings very clear: She hated everyone on sight.

Sooty simply stayed away from her. The rest of the family did, too. But I kept trying to tame her. Day after day, I held Miss Kitty on my lap, gently stroking her, and she usually accepted the attention for a time. When she decided she'd had enough, though, she gave no warning. She just flipped over onto her back, clamped her teeth down on the offending hand, and raked the attached arm with her back claws. I often went around with hands and arms that resembled pin cushions.

Miss Kitty was grown before she had another experience to justify her dark view of humans. She had brought an early-summer litter of kittens into the world in a corner of what my family called "the entry." It was a small enclosed porch leading to the kitchen door, the most accessible entrance to the house and the only one anybody used. The corner was a well-protected place to harbor mother and babies. The outer door to the entry always stayed open, which meant that Miss Kitty could come and go as she pleased, and a rug under a small table that stood behind the open door provided a cozy corner cave.

Miss Kitty loved those kittens fiercely and took excellent care of them. But it happened that our family was going on vacation while the kittens were still very young, so Hugh asked Brad, a friend and neighbor, to take over his paper route and, while he was doing that, to come by and feed the cats every day. Brad agreed, and we went off on our trip.

We returned two weeks later to find the entry littered with smashed flower pots tipped from a high shelf, the kittens gone, moved to the woods, we later found out, and a Fuller Brush catalog stuck between the inner screen door and the door that led into the kitchen. We pieced together the first part of the story from the evidence on hand.

The Fuller Brush man had come by and, finding no one home, put his catalog between the two inner doors and left, shutting the solid outer door to the small porch behind him. Obviously, he'd forgotten that the outer door always stood open, and he probably never saw the cat and her babies in their dark corner. He must have had no idea that he was shutting the mother in, away from the food and milk Brad set out each day beneath a nearby tree. Away from the small creatures she hunted, away from places distant enough from her brood to safely relieve herself.

Miss Kitty had clearly gone crazy.

The rest we learned from Brad. He had arrived one evening, pausing on the paper route to feed the cats, only to find the door to the entry firmly closed and Miss Kitty, frantic at her confinement, leaping and yowling and scrabbling inside. Of course, he opened the door. Wouldn't you? Simply releasing a trapped cat seemed the way to proceed.

But this wasn't just any cat. It was Miss Kitty. And she had never been much impressed by kindness. So instead of responding with gratitude toward her benefactor, she flew at him in a rage. She attacked Brad so fiercely that he gave up on the idea of feeding her and ran down the hill behind the house with the canvas bag of papers banging against his butt. "She was like a mad dog," he said, pulling down his sock to show remnants of the neat puncture marks on each side of his Achilles tendon. "She caught up with me and tore a big piece out of my sock!"

A neighbor, working in his garden at the top of the hill, heard Brad yell and ran over to help. For good measure, Miss Kitty chased him down the hill, too.

Brad was a loyal friend. He continued to bring food for the two cats until we returned, but each time he did, he tiptoed through the yard quietly, always relieved that he hadn't encountered the gray cat again. And when it came time to find homes for the new litter of kittens, he made a great point of saying they didn't need a cat at his house.

From that day on, Miss Kitty had a reputation in the neighborhood. She still tolerated the members of her immediate family, barely, but she looked at other human beings—especially males—with a distinctly jaundiced eye. She once allowed a visiting toddler who had escaped supervision for a few moments to haul her about without a sound of complaint or extended claw. But no one outside the family with an even slightly deepened voice or long trousers was permitted to come onto the property. A wandering dog that had the poor judgment to trot across our yard one afternoon was ridden into the woods with Miss Kitty attached firmly to his back.

Dad had never taken much interest in the gray cat—or

any of our cats, for that matter—but he did now. "We'll be sued, you know," he said to Mom, again and again. "If that cat attacks one more person, we'll be sued!"

Mother listened to his dire forecasts without comment. I listened, too, without paying much attention. Dad was a worrier. He always seemed to be fretting about something.

The truth was, though, as hard as I would have fought to keep her, I was half afraid of my beloved Miss Kitty. Even a task as simple as giving her a bowl of stinky cat food turned into a hazard. She didn't stay on the floor, mewing and rubbing and twining between my ankles, as any proper cat would do. Instead, every time I fed her, Miss Kitty threw herself into the air, snatching at the bowl—and at the vulnerable hand that carried it—with stiletto claws. And because her deadly exuberance put terror into my heart, I tended to put off the next feeding until she was so hungry that her leaping and grabbing and clawing was even more dramatic—and more painful—than the time before. Still, she was mine, and if her existence in our family had been threatened, I would have fought to keep her.

Or rather I would have until I saw the puppy.

I discovered the puppy the day I visited Mrs. Auger, a friend of my mother's who lived a mile or so farther out of town than we did. The Augers had taken in a stray mongrel, which had promptly produced a litter of puppies in their basement.

There were three of them, all black-and-white. Two had

smooth, short coats that barely seemed like fur; the third, a scraggly rough coat. Every one of them was ugly. They seemed to be constructed solely of mouths, round, fat tummies, and stick tails.

I fell in love. I fell so hard, in fact, that I rode my bike home at top speed and ran into the house, breathless, to make my announcement.

"Mrs.-Auger-says-that-I-can-have-a-puppy-if-you-say-it's-okay-so-can-I?"

It wasn't the first time I had asked for a puppy, so I knew perfectly well what answer to expect: *"Both your dad and I are at work all day, and you and Hugh are in school. There would be no one to stay home with a dog. Besides, even though we are on the edge of town, there are still leash laws here. A dog would have to be tied up all the time, and that wouldn't be fair."*

This time, though, Mother just said no. A flat *no,* without any explanation attached to it at all.

"But why?" I wailed. "Mrs. Auger says I can have one!"

My mother's face slammed shut.

The argument continued the next day and the day after that.

"Why can't I have a puppy?" I kept pleading. "It's not fair. I'll take care of him. I'll feed him and clean up after him and teach him everything he needs to know. Why can't I?"

"Because," Mother said finally—shifting tactics out of total exasperation, I'm sure—"you already have two cats."

This explanation stopped me like a brick wall. I looked

up from the bowl of ice cream I was mooshing with the back of a spoon to make ice-cream soup and held myself perfectly still. *That's what's keeping me from having a puppy? The second cat?* And in that instant, Miss Kitty's fate was sealed.

When I spoke again, it was slowly and carefully, though I knew perfectly well that my suit had little chance. Still, I lined the words up one after the other in precise order, like tenpins that I hoped could escape being knocked down. "If I gave away one of the cats . . . if I gave away Miss Kitty . . . could I have a puppy then?"

My mother, standing at the sink scrubbing potatoes, didn't answer.

"Could I?" I begged.

Still no reply.

"Mom?"

"We'll see," she said finally. Flat. Utterly noncommittal.

I knew. I was twelve years old, and in my deepest heart I knew that my mother would never let me have a puppy. But it was the closest I had ever come to the answer I wanted, so I chose to believe she would. I rose from my place at the table and whirled about the sunny kitchen.

"I'm going to have a puppy," I announced as I spun past my skeptical-looking brother, who had just appeared in the doorway. "A real puppy!" I flung a leg out in one direction, an arm in the other in an arabesque. Hugh shook his head and continued on his way to the living room to listen to *The Lone Ranger* on Dad's console radio. Miss Kitty, who happened to be stalking through, hissed at my swinging leg. Then she pushed out the screen door and let it bang shut behind her.

I went on dancing, hugging myself ecstatically and crooning, "A puppy! A puppy! I've always wanted a puppy."

Mother didn't say another word.

Everything was settled. Mom had found a farmer who would take Miss Kitty. The farm was miles away, far enough that Miss Kitty wouldn't know where she was in relation to our house and would be sure to stay. Mother told me what a good life cats had on a farm. All that milk. A warm barn to sleep in. I wanted the puppy desperately, so I tried hard to believe her.

When the day came to deliver Miss Kitty to the farm, Dad was at work at the mill, so Mom drove our black '36 Ford. Hugh rode in the front with her. I sat in the back with Miss Kitty next to me on the seat in a cardboard box. From the moment she had been stuffed, struggling, into the box, she seemed to know that something terrible was going to happen. She yowled, a deep, throaty wail I'd never heard from her before, and clawed at the folded flaps of the box. I kept talking to her and trying to stroke a paw each time one emerged through a crack, but that cat was smart . . . and entirely unreformed. The instant she felt a touch on the back of her paw, she'd twist it around to try to catch the offending finger with her claws.

I suppose I could have predicted what happened at the farm—if I'd let myself think about any of it beforehand, that is. I got out of the car with Miss Kitty, released from the box and held tightly against my chest, and two big farm dogs came lolloping up to us, barking cheerfully. (Hugh remained inside the car with his door firmly closed.) Miss Kitty, unconvinced by the dogs' good cheer, clawed her way out of my arms and over my shoulder, leapt to the ground, and disappeared into the cornfield next to the driveway.

I cried. What else was there to do? My mother tried to reassure me, telling me Miss Kitty would come back to the barn, telling me again about the good life a cat has on a farm. But I knew perfectly well that my cat had no reason to relate to that particular farm or to know that the people there intended to feed her and take care of her. And with those big dogs around, there was no reason to think she would ever return to the farm, either. Some things I could choose to believe, just because I wanted to, but others were beyond even my powers of self-deception.

I cried and cried. Halfway home I finally stopped long enough to ask, my voice still dripping accusatory tears, "Now can I have my puppy?"

Mother didn't answer. I studied the back of her head as she drove, but the back of her head showed nothing. She gazed out through the windshield as though driving took every ounce of her concentration. But when I began whining and begging, reminding her that she had "promised," she finally spoke.

She said, "No." Just that. Another flat, bald *no*. No explanation. No apology. Just *no*.

Hugh turned around in his seat and grinned at me. It was an I-told-you-so grin, though he had never told me anything. The truth was, he hadn't needed to.

Mother's answer was what I had expected all along. I wasn't dumb, whatever my brother may have thought, just eager to believe, in the face of all logic.

I understood, at last, what I had avoided looking at until then. My mother had manipulated me to get what she wanted . . . to be rid of my cat. A cat I now loved utterly, whatever her faults. I cried harder.

They were no longer tears of self-pity and loss, though. They were tears of rage.

A week passed. School started, both for Hugh and me as students and for our mother as a kindergarten teacher. It was 1951, and I was in eighth grade now. I grieved over Miss Kitty every day, especially before I fell asleep at night, wondering where she had gone after she leapt into that cornfield, wondering if she could still be alive. I also grieved about the puppy that would never be mine. But by the time Saturday dawned, sunny and with just a hint of fall snap, I put such thoughts aside and went off to my dance classes in Lafayette. And because I wasn't there that day, wasn't even thinking about Miss Kitty, the rest of this story must be imagined.

During the school year, Mom always did laundry on Saturday, so she was probably outside, pegging wet clothes to the line, when it happened. As soon as she'd hung this load, she may have planned to dig a few potatoes for supper.

In my imaginings, she had just folded a wet sheet, snapped it into submission, and attached it to the line with three pins when she turned to see a gray cat stomping toward her across the fading grass. The creature was bedraggled and bony and one ear was torn, but there could be no confusion about it. The cat was Miss Kitty. The look of pure hatred in her yellow eyes was unmistakable.

I suppose Mother's first thought was, *Thank goodness Claire isn't here to see!*

And let's say, too, that at the same moment Hugh came around the corner of the house, a baseball glove on one hand, a ball in the other. When he saw Miss Kitty, he must have stopped walking—simply halted as though he had come up against a pane of glass—and stared, first at the cat, then at our mother, waiting to see what would happen.

"Don't tell Claire!" she most likely commanded before hurrying into the house to make a phone call. Then she wrestled the cat into another cardboard box, and with Miss Kitty yowling once more from the back seat of the car, she drove off.

Why? I can only assume my mother didn't want to face me again with the solution to the problem of the obnoxious cat unraveled. No doubt she'd just had enough. Enough cats. Enough of my begging. Enough of my dad's endless talk about being sued. He talked and talked about all the terrible things that could happen, but she was the one who was expected to come up with solutions.

Besides, it was true that Miss Kitty might have gotten

them into trouble one day, despite the fact that locating a lawyer and suing would probably be the furthest thing from the minds of most folks in that working-class community. And if Miss Kitty did cause trouble—whatever the trouble might be—Dad would no doubt say that it was all Mother's fault. He would say she hadn't listened. How she must have wished sometimes that it was possible *not* to listen.

The farm Mother went to this time lay on the other side of the Illinois River. I can imagine the scene easily: My mother and the farm wife—the mother of one of her former kindergartners—carrying the box into the tack room in the barn, settling it gently on the floor, and putting a bowl of milk down beside it. Maybe Mom had even been so generous as to bring some cat food with her— something a cat in a barn hardly needed. Then the two women would have slipped out, closing the door firmly behind them.

And if Miss Kitty chose not to stay in this good place, the Illinois River was certainly wide and swift enough to stop any cat, even one as fierce and determined as she.

It took Miss Kitty exactly two weeks to turn up at the house again, looking more bedraggled and, if possible, angrier than before. This time Hugh was the one who saw her first. He was sitting on the back steps reading a *Superman* comic when the gray cat marched across the slag road and up the concrete walk to the door. (Once more I was in Lafayette at my dance lessons, and thus out of the story.) Hugh studied the scruffy cat long and hard; then he called to our mother.

Now . . . right here, I'd like very much to say that when Mom gazed at the poor beast, her heart softened. After all, Miss Kitty had struggled through many miles and across a wide river to return to the place that had once been her safe haven. Who wouldn't have been moved by such loyalty and determination?

My mother, that's who. She was—as my father was fond of saying—a very stubborn woman. Once she made up her mind, it stayed made up.

Even so, perhaps she actually did pause, just for a moment, to reconsider. And then—because this story must go where it must go—maybe it was Miss Kitty who sealed her own fate. Such sealing is easy to imagine: Mom bending to give the cat a resigned but welcoming pat, Miss Kitty reaching out with unsheathed claws to slash at my mother's face. If the way I imagined it were true, you would agree my mother had no choice, wouldn't you? And then, of course, you would have to understand why she did what she did.

I would have to understand, as well.

But the truth is, that's not the way my brother relayed that part of the story. I've even tried telling myself that he simply left those kinds of details out. He is, after all, a just-the-facts-ma'am sort of guy, and perhaps he failed to report such a compelling moment. But if that's true, then it's true also that my imagination refuses to fill it in.

What I do know is that my mother did not want to face

either my father's dire warnings or my inevitable and impassioned defense of that horrible cat. What I know, too, is that she had run out of options for finding a home for Miss Kitty that would be remote enough to keep her from coming back. And what I am absolutely certain about—because Hugh told me—is what she did next. She got rat poison.

From where? He didn't say. Did she keep such a thing in the pantry? Or did she climb, once more, into our old Ford and drive into town?

What was she feeling? Sad? Triumphant? Resigned? And if she had to drive into town, what might she have said to the grocer or the druggist, whoever in our small town sold such a brutal thing, when she paid her bill? Did she comment pleasantly on the weather?

And did Hugh object when he saw what she was going to do?

Maybe he did and she ignored him; I don't know.

Perhaps she said to herself simply, "These kids just don't understand." On the farm, she had grown up knowing that animals die. All her girlhood she had raised calves, fed them and bathed them and brushed them and, yes, loved them, so they could be shown at the 4-H fair and afterward sold for slaughter.

Did she remind herself of all the calves she had loved before they died?

I don't know, but what I do know for certain is that she stirred rat poison into a bowl of cat food and then called Miss Kitty into the house.

Hugh may have hovered behind her, saying, "You know Dad worries about things that won't ever happen. Nobody around here is going to sue us."

And as was often her habit, I'm guessing my mother didn't answer.

She just held the poisoned food high and made her way down the basement stairs. And this is a moment I don't have to imagine. I know exactly how Miss Kitty responded—leaping and yowling and clawing at the bowl even before it was on the floor.

Hugh was standing at the top of the stairs when she climbed them and returned to the kitchen. She didn't look at him, just said, "Close the basement door."

Hugh closed the door and went back outside. Alone in the kitchen, my mother listened to Miss Kitty die.

The poison did not work gently. Soon the cat was moaning, then yowling. The yowl turned into a scream. Mother stayed in the kitchen, right above the sound. She had decided to make her famous rhubarb cake. Everyone in the family loved her rhubarb cake . . . especially me.

Even after Miss Kitty finally went quiet, Mom must have waited a long time before she opened the door at the top of the basement stairs. But at last she had no choice. I would be home soon.

When she first looked through the doorway, when she walked cautiously back down the plank stairs, she could see nothing, though the basement light was on. She had left it on the whole time, as though a cat needed light to die.

Then she saw her. Miss Kitty was lying between the furnace and the wall. However the rat poison had worked—and I'm guessing my mother hadn't really asked herself how it would work—the cat had inflated like a balloon. Everything about her was round and tight, so that her legs stuck out in four different directions.

Mother opened the door to the furnace. *Thank goodness*, she must have thought. *Daddy*—that's what they called one another in those years, Mommy and Daddy—*fired up the furnace last night.* Then she stood, looking down at the creature. She probably wished she had something to pick it up with . . . even a dishtowel would have helped. But then, if she used a dishtowel, it would be like throwing a perfectly good towel away. She would never be able to use it to dry dishes again.

Finally, she took a deep breath and reached for one leg, then another. Just as she did, the door opened at the top of the stairs and she leapt away, dropping the carcass, as though she had been caught in some shameful act.

Hugh stood at the top of the stairs.

"Go away," she said, and without a word, he closed the door.

Again she picked up the cat that was no longer a cat, no longer anything, and thrust it into the mouth of the furnace.

Would Daddy notice—charred bones, perhaps, or scraps of fur—when he shoveled out the clinkers? Would she have to tell him what she had done? He wouldn't want to know, of course. He wanted the cat to be gone, but he wouldn't want to know how it had been accomplished.

My mother put in another scoop of coal so the fire would burn hotter.

Then she closed the furnace door, adjusted the damper, and went upstairs to start dinner for her family.

I don't remember how much time went by before Hugh finally broke his promise to Mother and told me what had happened to Miss Kitty. Maybe a year passed. Perhaps more. By the time our conversation occurred, I had quit thinking about Miss Kitty, quit grieving over the sight of her disappearing into the cornfield, quit wondering what terrible thing might have happened to her. I'd almost quit thinking about the black-and-white puppy, too.

It was high summer when Hugh told me—I'm certain of that—because I remember we were both sitting on the back steps, licking Popsicles. They were banana Popsicles. I remember that, too. A brand-new flavor.

Who knows why Hugh decided to break his promise that day? Was it out of a sense of justice—not wanting me to be left in the dark? Or maybe he was annoyed with me and simply wanted to twist my emotional arm in a big-brotherly way. Anyway, he told me all of it, everything that had been kept hidden from me. How Miss Kitty had come home, not once but twice. How she had come home even from the other side of the Illinois River.

I listened, amazed. How had my cat known where to go? To this day, I cannot figure out how she crossed the river. Did she walk across the highway bridge, dodging cars? Or leap from tie to tie on the bridge that carried the railroad track? Did she swim?

Then he went on to tell me how our mother got rat poison, how she mixed it into the cat food, how she fed my ravenously hungry cat. And how Miss Kitty had howled down there in the basement. He even told me how she looked at the end, like a furry basketball with all four legs sticking out in different directions. And about how he'd heard the furnace door clink shut. After he said that last part, about the furnace door, he fell silent.

I sat holding the bare stick from my Popsicle. I'd held it tight the whole time he'd been talking, watching it drip into a yellow puddle.

When Hugh spoke again, he said, "You've got to promise not to tell her I told you."

Promise? Promise? I was filled with unspeakable rage. A stronger, more profound rage, even, than the one I'd felt when I'd realized my mother had used my longing for a puppy to trick me into getting rid of my cat.

She had killed Miss Kitty. Killed her! How could I ever forgive her? And how could I forgive Hugh for bringing me the news?

Still, I looked over at my brother, sitting beside me on the back steps. His Popsicle had also dripped into a small yellow puddle on the sidewalk. And I thought, *He feels bad about Miss Kitty, too. He's probably the only person in the world, besides me, who ever cared about her.*

"I promise," I said finally. "I'll never tell her."

And I never did.

———

Even today, I sometimes think about that angry, determined cat, struggling to reach home, and I live through the whole story again. My brother's rescue of the abandoned kitten, my mother's "solution" for the obnoxious cat, Hugh's revelation that I didn't need to hear. Mostly, though, I think about my own complicity, about my eagerness to sacrifice the gray cat for an ugly black-and-white puppy that I knew in my deepest heart would never be mine.

And then, I think about my mother. How alone she must have been—how fiercely and completely alone—the day she killed Miss Kitty.

Sin

Father Gormley stood before the confirmation class, small and dapper in his immaculate black suit and his crisp, backward white collar. "Claire," he said. "Name the first of the three promises your sponsors made for you when you were baptized."

I closed my eyes and recited from memory the words from the Offices of Instruction in the *Book of Common Prayer,* saying them rapidly, so I wouldn't have to think about them. "That I should renounce the devil and all his works, the pomps and vanity of this wicked world, and all the sinful lusts of the flesh."

Father Gormley smiled and nodded, but my face burned anyway. *All the sinful lusts of the flesh!* Was there anything more embarrassing for a fourteen-year-old girl to have to say in front of her priest? Was being confirmed, the ceremony that would make me an adult in the eyes of the church, worth such humiliation?

There'd been a time when I hadn't a clue what "the sinful lusts of the flesh" might be. As an innocent ten-year-old, I'd once heard some older Catholic girls talking about "impure thoughts," specifically about having to confess theirs to their priest. I'd decided right then that it was a good thing I was an Episcopalian and didn't have to go to confession, because I wouldn't know what to confess.

To remedy this lack, the day I heard the girls talking I came home from school, went directly up to my room, and closed the door. No longer would I be burdened with such innocence. I intended to have myself some impure thoughts.

I thought about boys and the *thing* they seemed so foolishly fond of. A weenie, we called it. I wondered, beyond the neat trick of being able to pee standing up, what a weenie was good for. I even thought about standing to pee myself, but I'd already tried it once and had only ended up making a puddle on the floor in front of the toilet. Was thinking about peeing an impure thought? I didn't know.

I thought about my . . . but I had no name for it. *Thing* didn't even fit. There didn't seem to be enough to what was between my legs to qualify for even that simple term. "Down there" was the way my mother referred to it. "Wash yourself down there." But there wasn't much to think about that, either. It produced pee, albeit from an uninspired sitting posture, and that brought me back to the same question: What was an impure thought, anyway? Maybe I should think about pooping. That was probably worse.

Next I thought about the time under Kenny's porch, only that was an impure *deed,* wasn't it? Not just a thought. I'd promised Kenny I'd show him mine if he'd show me his, and he did. I took a good long look, then crawled out from under the porch and went home. Sitting on my bed in my closed room that day, it occurred to me for the first time to wonder which was the greater offense: the sin of breaking my promise or the one I would have committed in keeping it?

All this thinking had taken only a few minutes, and once it was finished, I couldn't come up with another thought to think, impure or otherwise. So there was nothing left to do but go down to the kitchen for a snack. Impure thoughts, I'd decided, were seriously overrated.

Now, though, I was fourteen, and my world had changed profoundly. Now I knew all about the sinful lusts of the flesh. It was the stirrings of my body that were impure. It was *I* who was impure.

"Claire?" Father Gormley had come back to me again. Why did the confirmation class have to be so small? And why was it that Linda and Johnny, the other two kids being confirmed, always got the short, easy questions?

"Yes?" I said, hoping he would repeat his question, since I hadn't heard a thing he'd said.

"Are we Catholic or Protestant?" he asked.

I knew this one, too. "We are both," I said. "We protest the authority of the Pope, and we are part of the One, Holy, Catholic and Apostolic Church."

"And what does that mean?" he asked, looking beyond me to Johnny.

I supplied the answer inside my head. *It means the apostles mashed their hands on the heads of other people to make them bishops, and those bishops mashed their hands on other bishops, and on and on until today,*

*because of all that hand mashing, our bishops go back to
the apostles in a direct line.*

"Define sacrament," Father Gormley asked Linda next.

"A sacrament," she recited, "is an outward and visible
sign of an inward and . . ."

But I had quit listening. I was wondering whether
Linda would come to my house on Saturday if I invited
her. We could quiz each other to make sure we had everything down for the service on Sunday. Father Gormley
had told us the bishop would make us answer questions
before he confirmed us, so we had to be prepared.

Father Gormley also said that after the bishop laid his
hands on our heads to confirm us, he would give us each
a slap. The slap was an important part of being confirmed. It made you a soldier for Christ, preparing you for
the blows that came to all good Christians and reminding
you that you must fight for your faith. I'd thought about
the slap a lot. Mostly I'd wondered if it would hurt and if
it would leave a mark. I wanted it to leave a mark. One
that would last for days and days. Then everybody would
know that I'd been confirmed.

Now Father Gormley was telling us how wonderful it
was to be confirmed, how good we would feel that day.
Confirmation, he said, was like being baptized again. We
would be pure, washed clean of all our sins! Sin was something rarely talked about in the Episcopal Church, but
even so, the idea of this ritual cleansing fascinated me.

Neat-o! I thought, as I'd thought a hundred times
before. I had already decided that once I was confirmed, I
would never sin again. Not ever. Not even with impure

thoughts—though, of course, now that I was thirteen, I knew what they were.

On Saturday while I waited for Linda to arrive—she had accepted my invitation, and her mother was driving her over to my house—I kept thinking about sin. I couldn't help it. If you were going to give something up for the rest of your life, you at least needed time to say goodbye. I decided that there were advantages to being Catholic. *Roman* Catholic, we were taught to say. Most of the girls I knew were Roman Catholic. If you were Catholic, the nuns taught you all about sin, so it was easy to know what to avoid.

If you were Catholic, you even had purgatory, a place to go to get rid of all your leftover sins before you could get into heaven. And even though we Episcopalians were both Catholic and Protestant, I didn't think we were Catholic enough to be sent to purgatory.

But if you were an Episcopalian, the whole idea of sin was rather vague. Getting forgiven wasn't easily defined, either. You couldn't just go to confession and be done with it. Instead, you went around all the time knowing you didn't quite measure up. I knew all about not measuring up.

I didn't get a chance to talk about any of that with Linda, though. When she arrived, she followed me upstairs to my room, and then we just kind of stood there, looking at each other. We'd been in Sunday school together since we were little kids, always Linda and Johnny

and me, but we weren't really friends. She had never been to my house before, and I had never been to hers.

"Do you want a snack?" I asked at last, when the silence was too much to bear.

"Sure," she answered. Relieved to have something to do, I led the way back down to the kitchen. I got out bottles of Dad's Old Fashioned root beer and vanilla ice cream and set about making black cows.

"Let's get the studying over with," Linda said, taking a sip of her black cow and delicately wiping away the foamy moustache that clung to the soft little hairs on her upper lip. "Then we can do something fun."

So we went back up to my room and plowed through the Offices of Instruction. By the time our black cows were gone, we'd recited the answer to every question twice, and Linda was clearly getting bored and restless.

"What are we going to do now?" she asked, and since I was the hostess, I knew it was my responsibility to come up with an idea.

I scanned my mind, searching at ultra-high speed for something good . . . something better than studying. Better, even, than talking about sin. I stumbled upon a perfect idea, then hesitated. What if Linda thought it was wrong? But even if she did, I decided swiftly, even if she thought it was so wrong as to be a sin, we were both going to be wiped clean the next day. Weren't we?

"I know," I said, speaking with the kind of vigor meant to move right past such questions. "I know exactly what we can do."

We were alone in the house. My parents were shopping and wouldn't be home for another hour or so. And Hugh wasn't home either. So my plan was perfect.

This was modern times, the spring of 1953, and Osborne had recently put in the latest phones, the kind with a rotary dial. That meant you could make a phone call without having to talk to an operator—if it was local call, anyway. And all calls between the towns in the tri-city area, Lafayette-Pearson-Osborne, were local.

"Come on," I said, and I led the way back downstairs to the dining room, where the phone waited beside a stuffed chair with a gray slipcover.

I handed Linda the phone book. "Look up a name, any name," I instructed, "and give it to me with the phone number."

Linda, still obviously a bit bored, began flipping through the phone book. "Uh . . . ," she said, running her finger down a page, "Polski. George Polski." And as she read out the number, I dialed it.

A woman answered. "Is Uncle George there?" I asked, making my voice sugary sweet.

"Who?" she asked.

"Uncle George. My uncle George." I let myself sound a bit impatient, as though she should have known who Uncle George was.

"No," she replied, sounding confused. "He's not here."

"Oh," I said. "Well . . . then would you give him a message for me?"

"Yes," she said, though she still sounded tentative.

"This is Barbara. Barbara Polski? I'm his niece, and I'm

coming for a visit. A nice long one. I'll be on the train from Chicago that arrives at the Lafayette station at seven thirty-one tonight."

"But . . . but . . . ," the woman who must have been Mrs. Polski stammered. "He doesn't have a niece named Barbara. I'm sure he doesn't. We haven't been married very long, but I've met his whole family."

"Of course he has a niece named Barbara!" I replied, sounding shocked to my bones at this betrayal, and then I continued, the words tumbling out in rapid succession. "Hasn't he told you about me? I'm sure he must have told you about me. My daddy had to go away, and he said I could stay with Uncle George while he's gone. He told me Uncle George is a good man and that he'll take care of me. He promised that Uncle George would take care of me!"

"But he's not here!" Mrs. Polski wailed. "He's away on business. What should I do?"

The answer to that was easy. "Meet me at the train depot! Just think of how angry he'd be if you left me with no place to go."

There was a long silence, and then the woman said, her voice tightly controlled, almost quavering, "Barbara?"

"Yes?"

"Seven thirty-one, you say? At the Lafayette depot?"

"Yes."

"I'm your aunt Ruth, and I'll—I'll be there."

"Thank you, Aunt Ruth," I said, very solemnly before hanging up the phone.

Linda had watched this whole charade with eyes wide

and mouth slightly ajar. I'd winked once, and she'd smiled . . . almost.

After I hung up, with Aunt Ruth all set to be at the Lafayette depot that evening to meet the seven thirty-one train, I burst out laughing. "Oh," I said. "Wasn't that funny?"

And it was. Much funnier than the other telephone jokes I'd heard. "Hello. Is your refrigerator running? Well, you'd better hurry up and catch it." Or, "Is Mr. Wall there? No? Then what's holding up your ceiling?"

Linda laughed . . . at last. "You're good!" she said. "You're really good!"

I could feel myself growing taller. "You do the next one," I offered, feeling magnanimous.

But Linda shook her head almost violently, her long brown hair swinging. "Oh, I couldn't. You're so good at it. *You* do another."

And that was the way the rest of the afternoon was spent. We must have called half a dozen homes. Maybe more. I say "we," but I did all of the calling. Linda just looked up names and fed them to me. By the time we were done, I had an uncle John, an uncle Bob, an uncle Raymond, two uncle Joes and, of course, Aunt Ruth, all set to meet the seven thirty-one P.M. train out of Chicago.

Sometimes I made my voice sound like a young woman's, sometimes a little girl's, but I was always Barbara. Barbara and whatever last name theirs might be. I described myself, too. The same description every time: curly red hair, green eyes. I told them I'd be wearing a green jacket. The green in the jacket brought out the color of my eyes. I always said that—about how the green matched my eyes.

I slipped up once and started giggling while I was talking to Uncle Raymond. Linda, who'd been sitting there, hanging on to every word, began to giggle, too. I almost hung up, knowing I'd blown it, when "Uncle Raymond" began trying to comfort me. Apparently, my helpless giggles sounded like tears on his end.

And we were off and running again.

"Oh," Linda said, when I'd hung up the phone for the last time, "how I'd love to be at the depot tonight to see all those people trying to meet you."

And that was when my second idea arrived from on high . . . or from wherever such ideas come.

After supper, when it was time to take Linda home, Dad volunteered to drive us. My father is a difficult person to encapsulate in a story. He was scary in some ways. He could be angry, petulant, often gruffly critical. But he could also be generous and kind. He was almost endlessly available, for instance, to drive me and my friends wherever we might need to go. So I dared to hope that this evening he would be available for a brief detour.

"Dad," I said, once we were on our way to Pearson, where Linda lived. "Would you mind going by the train depot on your way? Just for a couple of minutes?" (Pearson was beyond Lafayette and the depot.)

"Why should I?" he demanded to know.

Linda threw me a frightened glance.

I ignored her. "Well, Linda was there yesterday. She went to the depot to meet her grandparents, you see, because they were coming for her confirmation. And she thinks she might have left her sweater in the waiting room."

"Might have?"

"She's looked and looked, but she can't find it anywhere else," I continued in a rush. "It was a really good sweater. Pink cashmere with a design made out of pearls on the front." Then I added, remembering that Dad probably wouldn't know what cashmere was, or care, "It's a really expensive sweater." Expensive he would understand. My father positively hated the idea of anything—especially something unimportant like clothes—being expensive.

By this time Linda was nearly hyperventilating at my side. She rolled her eyes and lifted one hand to signal me to stop.

"Do you mind, Dad?" I pleaded, still ignoring her.

He shrugged, his gaze intent on the road. "If she was so careless as to leave a good sweater at the train depot, it'll be gone by now. Someone will have taken it for sure." He paused, as though that was all he was going to say, and I held my breath. Then he added, with an air of resignation and disgust over careless people who leave expensive sweaters lying around, "I suppose we can stop by so she can check. But it won't be any use. I can promise you that."

I let out my breath and grinned at Linda. She slumped against the seat, limp.

When Dad pulled into the depot parking lot, we both jumped out of the car. "We'll only be a couple of minutes," I promised.

My father didn't reply, just tapped a Pall Mall from the pack of cigarettes he carried in his shirt pocket and got out his matches. We headed for the depot.

The station clock said seven forty-five when we arrived, and the room was empty.

"We're too late," I said, disappointment sweeping through me like an arctic wind.

But then I saw her, a woman entering the depot from the platform. She hurried toward us. "Barbara?" she called from halfway across the cavernous room, her voice too high, too bright.

Do I look like Barbara? I wanted to say. *Does either one of us look like Barbara? Red hair? Curly? A green jacket? Remember?*

But she kept coming. "I've been so worried," she was saying. "So worried!" Then, "I'm your aunt Ruth." And, to my astonishment, she enveloped me in a tight hug. Linda had entered behind me. Since "Aunt Ruth" was expecting only one girl, she didn't even seem to see that another was standing there in front of her.

"You *are* Barbara, aren't you?" she asked, leaning back so she could examine my face.

I shrugged and smiled in apology. She looked so hopeful that I would have turned myself into Barbara on the spot if I'd been able. "Uh," I said. "No. Not really. My name is Claire. Just plain Claire. Not Barbara."

I had heard the expression "her face fell," but I had

never truly witnessed such an event until that moment. As the woman stepped away from me, her face collapsed upon itself like a building imploding.

"I don't know what to do," she wailed. "Barbara called to say she was coming. She's my husband's niece. But she's not here. She said seven thirty-one. I'm sure she said seven thirty-one, and there wasn't even a train due in from Chicago at seven thirty-one."

It was then I noticed that she was wearing what must have been her best clothes to come to the depot to meet her husband's newfound niece. Heels and nylon stockings and a pretty pastel suit with a skirt that flowed almost to her ankles. She wore perfume, too—a flowery perfume that made my nose twitch. The hands she wrung were dressed in immaculate white gloves.

"George," she went on, "is going to be so upset. He'll tell me I can't do anything right. I know he will. That I can't even meet his niece at the depot and do it right. And I was so looking forward—"

Without a look or a word passing between us, Linda and I simultaneously turned and fled.

When the confirmees met at the church the next day, Linda and I didn't seem to have anything to say to each other. I wanted to say, very casually, "Wasn't that funny, what we did yesterday?" Emphasizing the *we*. But somehow nothing about our time together felt particularly funny any longer, and if she wasn't going to talk about it, well, then I wouldn't, either.

Anyway, I told myself, even if the game we'd played was a sin, we would both be as pure as cherubim and seraphim by the time the service was over. And since I didn't intend to do another telephone prank as long as I lived, I had nothing to worry about. So without even casting a glance in Linda's direction, I marched into our little church to be confirmed.

My first disappointment about confirmation had come long before the day itself. Mother wouldn't let me have a white dress—the perfect outfit in which to parade my newfound "purity" before the world. She said that white was neither practical nor pretty, so my dress was a soft plaid, orchid-and-pink. Linda's was pale pink; perhaps her mother felt the same way. Johnny wasn't dressed in white, either, except for his shirt, of course, beneath his navy blue suit. But then, boys weren't expected to be all in white. I guess "purity" wasn't so important for them . . . even symbolically.

The second disappointment came on the day itself. The bishop didn't ask us a single question. Not one. All our studying had been for nothing.

The third came at the actual moment of confirmation, or to be more specific, it came with the slap that Father Gormley had told us to expect. The bishop didn't slap us. I mean, not at all. We knelt there at the altar rail right in front of him, and he laid his hands on our heads firmly enough—I had to stiffen my neck against the weight of those big hands. But then, when it came time for the slap, he just cupped a gentle palm against my cheek for an instant and then moved on to Johnny. I was left kneeling there at the altar rail wondering what, if anything, had just happened.

And maybe that's why I did what I did—because of all those disappointments piling up, I mean. I knelt there in my orchid-and-pink plaid dress, and when the bishop removed his hand from my cheek, I looked over at Linda, my co-conspirator in sin, and something inside me burned with a quiet heat. Pure? I was now pure? If that was true, then why could I still hear that quavering voice calling to me from across the train depot? Why could I see "Aunt Ruth" hurrying toward me? And why did I find myself wondering, even now, what she had said to her husband when he got home . . . and what he had said to her?

Strangely, in that moment, I could no longer remember why I'd wanted so badly to have all my sins forgiven. So that when I died, I could go to heaven? The one my dad, who never went to church, said was "all a bunch of hooey"? The one my mother once told me didn't accept cats? Not even my sweet Sooty, lying in a silent heap under the porch where she had crawled to die after being mauled by a neighbor's dog?

Maybe, I told myself, *there really isn't such a thing as "pure" . . . not as long as you can still remember.*

And maybe, just maybe, I didn't *want* to forget my sins!

So I did it. Kneeling there in front of the blessed sacrament with the bishop cupping a gentle hand to Johnny's cheek and Father Gormley standing at his side, all important in his satin vestments, I found myself wondering if I still could. Sin, that is. So I tried it out, just to see. In my newly purified state, I committed the worst sin I could think of.

I swore. But not so anyone could hear.

Inside my head I said, very loudly, "Hell!" Then I said, "Damn!" And then I added the worst swear I knew, the one my father sometimes used. "God damn it all to hell!"

I held my breath, waiting for something to happen—something terrible.

Nothing did.

When I stood to return to my place in the pew, along with Johnny and Linda, I thought, *Well. Purity doesn't last very long, does it?*

But you know what? I was content. A little guilty in a familiar way, but, nonetheless, content. In fact, I felt very much like the girl I wanted to go right on being.

Everything We Know

I

Everyone knew Billy Simmons was, well . . . you know . . . *that way.* I say we knew, though I suspect that in 1953 few people in our collection of small towns had a word—not a nice one, anyway—to describe what was so apparent to us all. Forced to describe Billy, we would have said he was queer or a fairy or. . . . The choices went sharply downhill from there.

It is true that Billy fit every stereotype. He was fine-boned, slender, handsome almost to the point of being pretty, graceful, a good dancer. He taught me how to jitterbug. His favorite activity in spare moments was to design elaborately flowing dresses for the emaciated women who emerged from his pencil. No wonder we thought he was . . . well, different.

Billy and I met our sophomore year in high school when we were both accepted onto the yearbook staff. The school was a large one, located in Lafayette. Students came together there from the entire tri-city area and beyond, so I made the move to high school with classmates from both of my former schools. Though my reputation as an outsider surely followed me, I found a safe harbor in the yearbook room. Billy probably felt the same way. Working on the staff meant we had a place where our talents could be used, even respected.

The two of us were in charge of the sophomore pages, selecting photos of our classmates engaged in their various activities, writing copy, laying out the class pictures and making sure they were all properly identified. Performing these tasks together, we came to be friends.

Our desks in the staff room—not the typical student desks lined up in rows, but actual working desks with kneeholes and drawers—butted up against each other, head to head, off to one side of the room. Other desks were similarly positioned around the room, where other students bustled with duties concerning different sections of the yearbook—the pages for the other three classes, sports, clubs, and special activities such as the prom. I can't imagine, though, that any of the other students could have been quite as happy to be there as Billy and I were. Every time we looked up from work, our eyes met in silent acknowledgment. Life was good. We had found a place where we belonged.

And there was something else we had in common. We were both very fond of Miss Yates, our faculty adviser. She was an English teacher when she wasn't advising the yearbook, though neither Billy nor I had ever been in one of her more traditional classes. But during seventh period, when the yearbook staff met, she became something much more than a mere teacher. She became our queen, and Billy and I were her devoted subjects.

I use the word "fond" to encompass what I assumed at the time to be Billy's level of affection, too, because he certainly liked and admired Miss Yates. The word isn't nearly strong enough to describe my feelings, though. I *adored* Miss Yates, and part of my reason for liking Billy so much was that he was the only person in the world willing to listen patiently while I babbled on about her virtues. He was so kind, in fact, that he never once referred to my ardor as a "crush," the term that would have fit all too well.

It wasn't Miss Yates's looks that captivated me, although she was nice enough looking in a thirtyish-schoolteacher sort of way. She had brown hair that she wore with the front rolled off her face into a sausage, a style that was rather old-fashioned even for that time. She had pale freckles, lots of them, a small but blunt nose, and glasses. She also had a nice figure, soft and curving in the right places, but the dresses she wore were appropriately teacherly, so her figure was pretty well disguised.

What I found especially compelling was the way she always stood close, not off at a distance, as other teachers did. I don't mean physically near, though it's true that she moved among us, bending over our desks, correcting something here, offering a suggestion there. What I mean is that she treated us like equals—a rare treat for a teenager in the 1950s. She even let us call her Shirlee instead of Miss Yates. Shirlee with two *e*'s. I thought that second *e* quite wonderful.

What most attracted me to Shirlee, though, was her intensity. When you spoke to her, whether about the earthquake that had just killed 1,500 people in Algeria, or about needing more rubber cement to dummy up a page, she listened with her entire being. Her eyes focused tightly on your face, and you were, at least for those few moments, the absolute center of the universe. I had never been the center of anyone's universe before, except perhaps my mother's—but that center had not held past my very early years. And I was, as yet, quite innocent of romance, so I hadn't experienced being that kind of center, either.

But from the very first day, I fell in love with the intensity of Shirlee's gaze. Certainly, there is no other way to describe what I felt, my heart's soaring when she walked into the room, its subsiding into a waiting quiet when she left. It was a love that grew steadily through my sophomore year. I went to sleep at night holding Shirlee's dear face, freckles, blunt nose, glasses—all of it—in my heart. And I woke each morning with her precious name—Shirlee, with two *e*'s, of course—on my lips.

Throughout that first year, I discussed with Billy every detail of Shirlee's wardrobe, her moods, the scraps of her private life we could glean. He was satisfying to talk to, because he not only listened, he added his own observations, commenting on her new earrings or suggesting something we might do that would please her—bringing her a bouquet of fall leaves or arranging all the books on her shelves in alphabetical order.

Over summer vacation, missing my daily discussions with Billy, I talked about Shirlee at home until my parents and brother rolled their eyes in exasperation. Then I arrived, breathless and expectant, in the yearbook room at the beginning of my junior year. Once more, Billy was there, too.

When the staff met on that first day of our junior year, Billy and I discovered we were the only ones to have a study hall scheduled for third period—which happened to be Shirlee's one block of free time. That meant we would be the only ones privileged to come in to give her extra help nearly every day, doing further work for the yearbook, and sometimes personal jobs like correcting tests for her English classes. Nothing could have been better . . . except, perhaps, if I alone had been available during Shirlee's free hour. But if I had to share her attentions with anyone, Billy would have been my first choice.

Of course, we both checked into study hall the next day and then checked right out again, arriving simultaneously in the yearbook room. Shirlee looked up and laughed at us, at our faces hovering over her desk like two bobbing balloons.

"Do you have any work we can do?" we asked in a single breath.

"Oh, sit down," she said. "Both of you. There'll be plenty of work coming up. For now, just sit."

We sat. I pressed forward expectantly, awaiting further instruction. Billy did, too.

Shirlee leaned back in her chair and clasped her hands behind her head. The movement lifted her breasts beneath her knit dress in a way I found disconcerting, though I didn't know exactly why. "Well," she said. "Are you glad to be back in school?"

"Oh, yes!" I burbled. Then I added, without meaning to, "It's really neat."

Instantly I wanted to bite off my tongue. Shirlee hated slang. She said words should be used with individuality and precision. She also said that listening to slang was like listening to the bellowing of a herd of cattle.

But if I wasn't up to the challenge of a first conversation with Shirlee, Billy was. He said, grinning mischievously, "The first days of school always remind me of being a little kid and getting a new box of crayons to eat."

Shirlee's eyebrows went up, and her sea-green eyes shone. "To eat?" she repeated.

Billy was clearly enjoying her rapt attention, perhaps nearly as much as I enjoyed it when it was directed at me, and I wanted to kick him and say, "Quit being so dog-goned charming!"

Oblivious to my unspoken command, he went on with his story, telling about how, when he was a little kid, every year he nibbled away at the new crayons his mother bought him for school. He'd eat one color at a time, always expecting purple to taste like grape, yellow like lemon, red like cherry . . . or perhaps strawberry, and so on. As he spoke, a dimple twinkled in his left cheek.

"What about the brown?" I asked, thinking dark thoughts about the possibilities. "What did you expect that to taste like?"

"Oh . . . brown!" Billy turned his grin on me, apparently reading my mind. But he answered, innocently enough, "Sometimes I was sure it was going to be chocolate, sometimes root beer." He turned his palms up expressively.

Shirlee leaned toward him. "And weren't you disappointed? Once you tasted them and found they weren't what you'd expected, you must have stopped eating your crayons . . . right?"

And off Billy went, describing the way he'd kept hoping, kept sampling, kept eating, until finally his mother refused to buy him any more crayons and got him colored pencils instead. "I was a very stubborn kid," he concluded. "But I never gave up hope, you know? Besides"—and he ducked his head in imitation of the shy little boy I was pretty sure he'd never been—"it was so much fun pooping all those wonderful colors."

I blushed. To use the word "poop" in front of a teacher—in front of Shirlee, of all teachers!

But Shirlee just sat back in her chair and clapped her hands. Her face had that full look you get after a good meal . . . or a good story.

In the silence that followed, I scrambled around in my head for a tale of my own, but I could come up with nothing . . . nothing nearly so cute, anyway. So instead I said, "I decided something this summer. I'm going to study journalism in college." I tried to sound casual, though I'd been waiting since early summer for a chance to tell Shirlee about my plans. For *this* chance. And her attention swung to me.

That's the way the whole period went, with each of us performing and Shirlee shifting back and forth between us in turn. I might have been annoyed with Billy for competing so well, except that each time Shirlee focused on me, the world righted again. When the period was over and we had to return to the ordinary demands of school, I floated into the hall. What a year this was going to be! How I loved that woman! In fact, at that moment I loved everyone . . . even my good friend Billy. As we moved down the hall, I bumped his shoulder in a comradely way, and he put one arm around me and gave me a warm, utterly platonic squeeze.

The next day, when the two of us showed up in the yearbook room during study hall, Shirlee had a surprise for us. She brought out two small cloth-bound books with blank pages. "You're both fine writers," she said. "I'd like to see you start keeping journals."

I held the journal in my hands as carefully as I might have held Shirlee's heart if she had handed it to me. No gift had ever been so fine. But it was Billy who asked the question that burned for both of us. "If we start keeping journals, will you read what we write?"

Shirlee straightened quite suddenly, as though the

question had startled her. Looking back now, I can easily imagine what must have flashed through her mind: those endless English papers, all the copy she had to read for the yearbook, the lesson plans to be prepared . . . and our scribblings, too? She must have thought her gift had turned on her. But she said only, "Don't you think a journal should be private?"

"Only if the person keeping the journal wants it to be," Billy argued.

And I bobbed my head in agreement. I couldn't imagine anything I could write—*anything*—that I wouldn't want Shirlee to read.

"*Well* . . ." Shirlee dragged the word out. "Okay," she agreed, finally. "I'll read some of it, anyway. Just put a star at the top of the pages that you especially want me to see."

We agreed. Both of us. What a perfect solution! And already the words of my opening pages were spinning in my mind. Lots of words. And lots and lots of stars.

From that day on, I was not only in love with Shirlee, I was in love with my journal, too. Writing had always been important to me, but writing for Shirlee was a deep and special thrill. I had no idea what Billy was doing with his journal. To tell the truth, I wasn't greatly interested. But I sat down to mine that first evening and poured out my heart. Shirlee had even chosen my favorite color for my journal, a rich amber, though I couldn't remember ever telling her it was my favorite. And each time I opened that golden brown cover, another conversation, one of the many I had long fantasized having with Shirlee, sprang onto the page almost without effort.

I wrote when I should have been doing homework. I wrote when I'd been told to go upstairs to clean my room. I kept on writing after I'd been called to the dinner table, and consequently ate more than one meal under the weight of my mother's silent disapproval. In my midteens, there wasn't much I did by halves, and writing for Shirlee's eyes was a recipe for obsession.

My journal opened this way:

I am a truth teller. That is, I firmly believe, my entire reason for being in the world . . . to discover the truth and to let it be known.

Adults lie about so many things . . . divorce, death, sex, Santa Claus. Maybe they lie about God, too. I've often wondered about that. Have you ever noticed the similarities between the story of God and the one about Santa Claus? How they are both "up there"—in the clouds, at the North Pole, not much difference—keeping track of everything we do, naughty or nice. But in the stories, it seems to be only the kids either one watches very closely. Grownups want us to believe that they're always nice.

I've got a lot of thinking to do yet, a lot of deciding. But I can't decide what I want to do with the rest of my life until I finish figuring out whether or not God is real. If He is everything everybody says, then I know exactly what I'll do. I'll enter a convent, the kind where all the nuns do the whole day long is pray. Because if I decide that God really did make us and that He truly is all-loving, all-knowing, all-powerful, if He exists, then the best thing I can do, the only thing I can do that matters, is praise Him . . . every waking minute. Because God is what being alive should be about.

But if I decide that God is just another Santa Claus, a skinny one surrounded by angels instead of elves, if I find out He's something you're suppose to believe in when you're a little kid and forget about after that, then I'm going to be mad. Really, really mad.

And then I'm going to become a reporter for the National Enquirer. I'll write stories about the end of the world as told by some guy who lived 10,000 years ago whose predictions have never gone wrong and about Martian babies born in Oklahoma. I'll write stories about God's being a fake, too. Or worse than a fake. About His never having been at all.

Because, you see, I'm a truth teller.

I wrote more passages like this, not just about religion, of course, but about all kinds of cows that seemed to be sacred to adults. Then I gave my journal to Shirlee and held my breath. I wanted, of course, for her to read—and love—every outrageous word. I knew she would. I even tried to honor her request to star only the entries I particularly wanted her to see. So finally, painfully, trying not to be greedy, I chose two short passages to be left without stars.

———

For three long days I watched Shirlee's face to see if I could tell whether she'd read my journal yet. I kept having second thoughts about some of the entries. *Maybe I shouldn't have said this. . . . Surely I shouldn't have written about that!* Shirlee was an adult, after all. Even she might be shocked by too much truth. Perhaps she might even be angry!

The day finally came when I arrived at the yearbook room—I always checked in there every day first thing in the morning—to find our journals back on top of her desk. She handed my amber one back to me, smiling. But she said only, "Nice. Write some more."

My heart stopped beating. "Nice" had been the furthest thing from my mind when I'd been writing. I had meant to write something so deeply insightful, so shockingly true that Shirlee's hand would tremble when she wrote at the bottom of the page, "Incredible! What insight! What a mature understanding of the world! What a flair for words!"

I took my journal back and leafed through it quickly. She hadn't made a single comment on any of the carefully filled pages that I'd marked with stars. Not even "Nice." The only words there were my own. I scolded myself silently. Shirlee had, after all, agreed to read parts of our journals, not to write comments in them. Anyway, she probably didn't want to spoil this record of our young lives with words of her own. Nonetheless, I was hurt.

Later, when Billy and I left the yearbook room together at the end of the day, I turned to him and asked, "What did Shirlee say to you?"

As usual, Billy was carrying his books against his chest the way we girls did, not at the end of his arm in a more manly grip, and he looked down at the journal stacked on top of the rest. (His was lavender, a color he'd seemed entirely happy with, though I can't help but wonder now whether the choice hadn't been just a bit ironic on Shirlee's part.) "She said, 'Nice,'" he replied.

"And was it?" I demanded to know. "Was your journal 'nice'?"

He smiled at me, and I couldn't tell if the smile was genuine or not. "Of course," he said. "Do you think I'd write anything for Shirlee that wasn't nice?"

I didn't know how to respond to that, so I said nothing.

We had walked a ways in silence in the midst of the throng of students, all pushing toward their lockers or the front door, when Billy added, "Do you suppose she actually read them?"

His question couldn't have shocked me more deeply if he'd asked if I thought she used our pages for toilet paper. "Of course she read them!" I cried. "Shirlee would never lie to us. You know that!"

"Sure," he agreed. "I know that." But he didn't sound entirely convinced.

In another week we both turned our journals in again, and again Shirlee took them cheerfully enough. This time I had moved on from challenging God to, far more daringly, I thought, challenging the entire educational establishment. *Surely she'll have something to say about that,* I thought.

Again, however, she returned my journal a few days later, practically without comment. All she said was, "You write well, Claire." I wanted to be angry. I tried, though I couldn't get beyond a brief fillip of irritation. In any case, I still refused to consider the idea that Shirlee might not actually be reading our journals.

When the third round went the same way, and then the fourth, my faith began to falter, just a bit. But then I opened my journal to the last page I'd filled—a hymn in honor of all the cats I'd known in my life—and saw it. A tiny beige spot in the middle of the page. A drip from a cup of coffee! It *had* to be coffee—something I never touched.

And so I flew to tell Billy. I found him just as he was checking out of study hall, heading for the yearbook room.

"Billy," I whispered fiercely, as we exited the large cafeteria that doubled as a study hall in our school—it was a Friday, and the smell of the fish sticks being prepared for lunch already hovered in the air—"Shirlee's reading our journals! I know she is!"

He looked skeptical, and something else I couldn't quite name . . . a bit worried, maybe? "How do you know?" he asked.

"Look!" I opened my journal to the anointed page and stabbed a finger at the pale beige spot.

Billy leaned over, peering at the book. "Well," he said finally, straightening up. "I guess you're going to have to tell me what it is I'm supposed to be seeing."

"That!" I said, holding my finger below the stain. Was it

possible it had grown paler since I'd first seen it? Could it be fading away? "That stain. Right there. It's coffee. I know it's coffee. And I don't drink coffee. I can't stand coffee. And no one else has been near this journal . . . not my parents, not anybody. So who else could have spilled that drop?"

We'd stopped in the middle of the empty hall, and Billy bent over the page again, studying it. He touched one slender finger to his mouth, then to the spot, then back to his mouth again. "You're right," he said at last, nodding solemnly. "That coffee has cream and sugar in it, just the way Shirlee drinks it. So that has to mean she's read every word."

It took several beats for me to realize that he was pulling my leg. "Oh . . . you!" I thumped him soundly in the middle of the back, remembering, even as I did, that sometimes, after all, I did drink hot chocolate and might have had a mug with me when I was writing.

We both laughed and headed out again. My perspective wasn't entirely gone.

We had just turned the corner to head down to the first floor and the yearbook room when two goons appeared. Their names were Hank and Jason, and though I'd never had much contact with either one, I knew them by reputation. Everyone did. They were what we called hoods. Hank was the worst. Jason, his sidekick, mostly just followed along, but that meant that he doubled every bad thing Hank said or did.

"Well, look who's here," Hank said, a grin splitting his beefy face. "What are you two girls doing out of class?"

Two girls. I avoided looking over at Billy to see how he was taking the insult.

"And look at the pretty pink book this one's carrying!" As he said "pretty pink book" Hank slapped Billy's journal off the top of the stack of books Billy had shifted to his hip. It splatted onto the floor.

"It's not pink," Billy protested, sweeping his journal up again. "It's lavender."

"Ooooh!" Jason said. "Did you hear that, Hank? It's *lavender!*" He drew the word out so that it sounded totally precious.

But Hank was not to be distracted by fine distinctions. "Let me see your book," he demanded, and he snatched Billy's journal from his hand, opening it so emphatically that the spine cracked.

"Give me that!" Billy cried, grabbing for it. But Hank was both wide and tall, and he easily held the journal out of Billy's reach. He opened the book above his head and turned it face-down so he could inspect the open pages. Helplessly, I looked up, too, not expecting to be able to read anything from that distance, but intent on willing Billy's journal out of Hank's hands.

The pages Hank had opened to didn't contain writing. They contained a drawing, instead—one of Billy's designer gowns. I could see, though, even from some distance that this dress didn't clothe one of his usual stick-like women. This model had curves, real ones. She also wore glasses and a familiar hairstyle, rolled away from her face. I couldn't help but wonder . . . did she have freckles, too?

And that's when I understood for the first time. Billy

wasn't just being kind about my infatuation. He was in love with Shirlee, too! I should have recognized the signs.

How could it be? How could fruity-fairy-queer-homo Billy be in love with my Shirlee? I'd never applied words like that to Billy before, not even in my mind, but now, suddenly, they fit. Or maybe, for the first time, I *wanted* them to fit.

Billy leapt again for the book, and a scuffle followed. His journal probably would have been torn—not to mention what might have happened to Billy himself—but for the fact that Mr. Trudell, the Spanish teacher, appeared suddenly from around the corner. Even hoods obeyed teachers in those days, at least when the teacher was standing right there in front of them, and instantly Hank dropped the book, which careened across the floor with Billy scrabbling after it.

When Mr. Trudell found out where Billy and I were heading and that we had permission slips, he sent us on our way. The other two, lacking either an appropriate destination or the proper slips, were still being dressed down when we reached the bottom of the stairs and turned the corner into the first-floor corridor.

I glanced over at Billy. His face was flushed. "Have those creeps messed with you before?" I asked.

He brushed off the sleeve of his pale blue sweater as though some remnant of Hank's touch still clung to him. "They've been at me since the day I walked into this school. One day I tried to punch Hank's face in, but I just hurt my hand. I think his head is made of stone."

I tried to imagine Billy going up against either one of those Neanderthals. I couldn't. I changed the subject. "Was that a picture of Shirlee I saw in your journal?" I asked.

"Well . . ." His face turned an even deeper shade of red. "I guess you could say some of my models might look just a bit like her."

I nodded, and after a few more steps asked, "And has she ever said anything to you about your drawings when she gives back your journal?"

" 'Nice,' " he replied. "She says, 'Nice.' "

We couldn't help it. We both laughed.

The answer to our question could hardly have been more clear. Presumed coffee stains with cream and sugar aside, our darling Shirlee wasn't even opening the journals she had promised so faithfully to read!

II

I asked myself over the next few days how Billy could be . . . well, as he was . . . and still be in love with Shirlee. But I always reminded myself that I was not *like that* at all and was of the same gender as Shirlee, and I loved her, too. So that, of course, settled the question. Besides, I wasn't an expert on men or boys of such a persuasion. For all I knew, they fell in love with inaccessible older women all the time.

I went on writing in my journal, and Billy, I presume, continued using Shirlee as a model. As daring as I had been when I was convinced Shirlee was going to read nearly every word that hit the page, I grew even more daring in my unasked-for privacy. And yet, the possibility that she might decide some day to do what she'd promised always hovered over every word I put down, keeping the process exciting. *Some day,* I kept thinking . . . *some day, she'll open this journal and begin reading and simply be unable to put it down.*

As disappointed as I was to realize that she hadn't kept her promise, my passion for Shirlee wasn't the least bit diminished, nor, as far as I could tell, was Billy's. She still listened when we talked to her, leaning forward almost breathlessly, her eyes wide. No one else in the world— certainly no other adult!—had ever found me so fascinating.

It was third period, a week or so after the discovery that our journals were more private than we would have liked, when Shirlee said, speaking mostly to the wall, but with Billy and me as her only audience, "I wish I had a smaller yard."

"Why would you want a smaller yard?" Billy asked, looking up from the freshman English tests he was grading.

She shrugged, smiled. "Maybe that's the wrong way to think about it. It's just that my back is sore, and I'm knee-deep in leaves. What I really wish is that I knew someone who liked raking."

Billy and I rose to the bait simultaneously. "I love to rake!" we both exclaimed.

Shirlee looked from one of us to the other with a surprised laugh, though I couldn't help wondering if she was really all that surprised. Surely she knew we were going to volunteer. Why else had she made the comment?

When school let out that Friday, we rode home with Shirlee. She lived alone, we discovered, in a small white house on a big corner lot less than a mile from the school. And she was right—the yard was practically knee-deep in crisp, colorful leaves.

Billy and I climbed out of the car and looked at the house, the yard, the leaves, and then at each other. I could tell that he was as pleased with the opportunity that lay before us as I was.

"First," Shirlee said, emerging from the driver's seat, "let's go in and have a snack. You'll need fortification."

And so she ushered us into her little house. The kitchen was small and cozy, with a rooster motif. She had roosters on her dish towels, a rooster on her toaster cover, colorful roosters strutting across the wall. Roosters were a popular kitchen decoration then, though there were none in my mother's kitchen. Mom, remembering chickens from her farm childhood, thought of them as dirty and didn't want them in her kitchen, even in the form of pictures, which just proved to me how up-to-date Shirlee was, how daring.

She served us cold milk and homemade peanut butter cookies. I wondered if she always had freshly baked cookies around or if she was so well-prepared because she'd counted on us to pick up on her hint. I brushed the thought aside. What did it matter? I was here, inside Shirlee's house, a place I'd never thought I'd actually see. I didn't want to stare, but I couldn't help looking around, trying inconspicuously to take in everything. I was going to absorb every tiny bit so that when I was home I'd be able to think about Shirlee in her domain, bustling around her tiny kitchen among her colorful roosters, relaxing in the easy chair I could just make out in the living room through the doorway . . . watching television, maybe?

I couldn't see far enough into the living room to see if there was a television set there. I guessed there probably was. We had finally gotten a TV at home the previous summer, and my dad had been one of the last holdouts against the new gadget. (He always said that if he wanted to watch snow he'd wait for winter and look out the window.)

When Billy and I finished our snacks, we went back outside and set to raking. Shirlee had two rakes waiting in the garage, one well-used and the other clearly brand-new. Again, her possessing a second rake gave me a moment's pause. After all, she lived alone and could hardly use two rakes herself. But I turned the implication aside. Shirlee had a right to own as many rakes as she wanted, didn't she?

Billy stood back to let me choose, and though I knew it was impolite to do so, I took the new one, remembering that Shirlee must have been thinking of me—or us, anyway—when she bought it.

The day was crisp, the leaves light and dry, the task easy. We had only to rake everything into a pile at the curb, and later we would have the fun of burning it. (There were no laws against burning leaves then.) Shirlee sat on the doorstep and talked to us as we worked, but after a while she went inside, saying she would be back out in a few minutes.

I remained in the front yard. Billy had begun to work his way around the side of the house. The tree shadows stretched out long as the sun dropped, and the air began to cool. About fifteen minutes later, having heaped everything we'd gathered from the front yard into the gutter along the street, I turned the corner of the house, too. It was a big yard; much raking remained to be done. At first I couldn't see Billy anywhere. Then I did.

He had stepped between some bushes alongside the house, whether in the pursuit of more leaves or for some other purpose I couldn't imagine. He stood perfectly still, the handle of his rake clutched to his chest in a tight embrace, facing a corner window. He was so totally absorbed in whatever was on the other side of that window that he was, as far as I could tell, completely unaware of me.

I moved closer, close enough so that I could see, too. And then I stopped, stunned.

The window Billy stood before looked into Shirlee's bedroom. Apparently, Shirlee hadn't noticed when she'd closed the drapes that one side had caught on something, leaving a triangular opening the full length of the window. And Shirlee was right there on the other side of the triangle . . . undressing!

Though I stood some distance behind Billy, the light in the bedroom was on, and I could see inside perfectly, probably almost as perfectly as he. Shirlee had removed the dress she had worn to school that day—the knit one I particularly liked because it showed off her figure so well—and now she stood in the middle of the room, covered only by a half-slip and a brassiere. The brassiere was the kind with circular stitching on the cups, and it thrust her breasts forward like twin rockets, poised for flight.

I knew I should step back, turn away, but I didn't. Couldn't. Instead, I remained rooted to the ground, holding my breath.

Billy must have been holding his breath, too, because he continued to stand as still as stone, his gaze fastened upon the window.

Shirlee wrapped her arms around herself in a hug and scratched her back as far as she could reach. Then she unhooked the brassiere and, leaning forward, slipped out of it. Her breasts, released from the white glow of the circle-stitched cups, swung lightly, softly. Her nipples were a rich, dark amber, and I could just make out a large birthmark, brighter than the nipples but very distinct, on the side of one breast. It was shaped like a butterfly. My hands itched to reach for the butterfly, as though to capture it before it took flight.

And that was the moment when Shirlee looked up, directly at the window. Her mouth fell open. Her face twisted with sudden, unmistakable anger, and she snapped to attention, covering her exposed breasts with crossed arms. I stepped back, silently, quickly, retreating around the corner. I didn't know whether Shirlee had seen me or not, but I was certain she had seen Billy.

Trembling, I went back to scratching at the already-cleared grass at the front of the house, my stomach twisted, my limbs weak. I was certain Shirlee would come bursting through the front door any instant, condemning Billy, condemning me!

Nothing happened. Nothing at all. I made my way back to the pile at the curb and set to work on making it higher, more compact, though all the vigorous raking I did produced little result. Everything I pulled to the top of the pile tumbled immediately to the base again. But at least I was nowhere near that window. "I'm innocent," my energetic motions proclaimed. "Don't blame me! I didn't see a thing."

After a few minutes, Billy appeared, pulling a pile of leaves toward the curb. He didn't look in my direction, and I decided he probably didn't know that I had stepped around the corner of the house, let alone stopped there to join him in his crime.

Time passed. I have no idea how much. An hour? Two? Probably more like fifteen minutes, but the minutes dragged by with excruciating slowness. Billy and I pulled at the dry leaves, tumbling them over one another so that they emitted a constant, accusatory rustle. My head lowered, I kept watch from beneath my brows on both the front door and Billy. The door remained closed.

Though Billy worked intently, his face impassive, his cheeks were splotched with red. *As well they should be!* I thought. I grew increasingly indignant, as though Billy, by infringing on Shirlee's privacy, had compelled me to do the same. But even as I proclaimed my innocence in my mind, my heart sent a message of truth to my entire body. "You are wicked," the steady beat accused. "Deeply, deeply wicked."

Fifteen long minutes. The sun had dropped behind the house across the street and the sky had faded to a pale pewter when Shirlee finally opened the front door and stepped out of her house. She wore slacks and a sweater. She must have put her circle-stitched brassiere back on—or a different one, perhaps—because I could see that her breasts, thrusting against the knit fabric, were firmly encased as breasts were always supposed to be in the fifties.

I waited, holding my breath. My bones had gone soft.

"I think it's time to take both of you home," Shirlee said without much inflection, and my heart sank. Then she had seen me, too!

We nodded, carried our rakes to the garage, and followed her silently to her car, a green Hudson that looked like an upside-down bathtub. Instead of scrambling as we had earlier for the honored place in the front, we both climbed into the back seat without a word.

"Tell me where your house is, Billy," Shirlee commanded, a stern gaze accosting him by way of the rear-view mirror. He gave her his address. It was in Lafayette, only a couple of miles in a different direction from the school.

She nodded, said, "We'll go there first," and pulled rather abruptly out of the driveway. Silence filled the car like cotton batting. It seemed to replace the air.

No one spoke all the way to Billy's house. He and I didn't even glance at each other. We both simply sat staring at the back of Shirlee's brown hair. The label of her sweater had pushed up beyond the collar, and I wanted to reach forward to tuck it in, but, of course, I didn't dare.

"Thanks," Billy said as he climbed out of the car. "Thanks for letting me help."

Shirlee nodded, still silent.

She sat at the curb waiting until Billy had disappeared through his front door, then she turned back to me and let out a huge breath. "Why don't you come up front, Claire?" she said.

My muscles managed to engage enough to get me out of the car and seated next to her. I couldn't look at her, though. Was she going to accuse me? If she was, why had she let Billy get off without a word?

She began driving again. "Do you want to get burgers at White Castle before I take you home?" she asked. Was it possible that her voice was actually friendly?

"Sure." I tried to sound enthusiastic, which I was, but my mouth was so dry that I had difficulty loosening my tongue to speak. Was it possible that Shirlee didn't know?

We went to the White Castle, got burgers, fries, a butterscotch milkshake for me, a strawberry malted for her, and sat down across from each other in a small booth. When I lifted the first fry to my mouth, my hand trembled, and I lowered it to the table again, waiting for calm . . . or at least the appearance of calm.

"Now," Shirlee said, fixing me with that wide-eyed gaze of hers. "Tell me what Billy was up to."

"Up to?" I repeated. "Was Billy up to something?" I sounded utterly stupid, I knew, but I didn't know how else to respond. If I admitted I understood what she was talking about, it was a very short step to having to admit that I'd been peeping, too.

Shirlee reached to cover my hand, the one holding the French fry, with her own. "You don't have any idea, do you? I should have realized that." She smiled at last, and her smile seemed relieved, if not exactly joyful.

I let a sigh slip out, carefully, inconspicuously. So she *didn't* know. For certain she didn't know. I was home free. Why, then, did I still feel so bad?

We sat in silence for a few more moments, eating our food. Despite the reprieve I'd just gotten, my stomach still clenched into a hard knot, hardly allowing the food admission. I kept at the meal valiantly, though, even tried to smile as I chewed.

When Shirlee spoke again, her voice made me jump. "I'll tell you what Billy was doing," she said. "He was peeping into my bedroom window when I was in there changing."

"Peeping? Really?" I asked. My voice creaked like an old woman's. And then I added, not knowing whether I was making excuses for Billy or accusing him, "I wouldn't have thought *Billy,* of all people . . ." But I let my words trail off. I was no longer sure what I had started out to say.

"I wouldn't have thought Billy, of all people, either," Shirlee remarked dryly. And then she laughed, a short, sharp burst.

After that we both just sat there, contemplating whatever it was about "Billy, of all people" that Shirlee's laugh had implied and that neither of us dared say.

I can't even guess what Shirlee was thinking during that moment of contemplation. I was thinking that Billy was my friend, that if he was going to have to take the rap for peeping, it was only right that I should take it with him. I had, after all, peeped every bit as hard as he. But the simple truth was that I couldn't. Or wouldn't. I wasn't about to risk losing Shirlee. She was what gave shape and substance and meaning to my days. And besides, I told myself . . . I really was innocent, wasn't I? I wouldn't have even thought to look toward that window if Billy hadn't been standing right there, staring.

What I didn't ask myself, what I never addressed then or for a long time after, was why I'd found it so fascinating to see Shirlee half-dressed, her breasts swinging free. After all, I'd been in locker rooms my entire life and had never paid any particular attention to the various states of undress of the girls and women around me. But then, everything about Shirlee fascinated me. So what was there to explain?

Shirlee drove me all the way home, even though I lived on the other side of the Illinois River, in Osborne, and buses traveled there on a regular schedule. She let me out in front of my gray frame house next to the cement mill.

"I'll be glad to come back and rake some more," I said as I stepped out into the crisp fall evening, grown entirely dark now. "I can take care of the pile we already have, too. We forgot to burn the leaves."

"That's nice of you," she answered, "but a friend is coming over this weekend. Dave can probably get the rest of it done."

A friend! Dave! So Shirlee *did* have a boyfriend. His name was Dave. I burned with sudden jealousy, a fiercer jealousy than I had ever felt over Billy's attentions toward Shirlee. Billy's difference, after all, kept him from seeming like serious competition. But a grown man—a *boyfriend!* Shirlee had never mentioned Dave before. I'd always thought of her as being entirely alone in her life, waiting, somehow, for me.

I turned back to her open window. "Still," I insisted, "if Dave doesn't get it all done, I'd be glad to come back and finish the job for you."

"I know you would," Shirlee said. And she reached out to brush my cheek lightly with the tips of her fingers, so lightly it almost wasn't a touch at all, yet my cheek burned with a fierce joy.

Then she drove away.

I stood in the red slag road and watched, then listened as her car crunched off into the darkness. *She knows!* my heart pounded in a steady beat. *She knows I love her, and it's all right!*

Why, then, did everything I felt seem so deeply and completely wrong?

III

The next Monday, I stopped by Billy's table in the study hall as I was taking the usual pass I'd gotten from Shirlee to the study hall teacher. Billy sat with his U.S. history text open before him. He didn't look up when I approached.

"Coming?" I whispered.

Without seeming to break his concentration, he shook his head.

I bent close. "Wouldn't Shirlee give you a pass today?"

His eyes still intent on a list of the causes of the Civil War, he didn't reply.

I put a hand on his shoulder. "Wouldn't she?" I hissed.

Billy marked his place on the page with a delicately tapered finger, then lifted his head to look at me for the first time. "I didn't ask," he said in a flat voice.

"Do you want me to ask? I'll get a pass for you and come back to get you."

Billy went on looking at me, his dark brown eyes utterly opaque. "No," he said at last, and he bent once more to his book.

I stood there for a moment, helpless. Shouldn't he at least try? And yet, if he went to Shirlee and she turned him down, that would be the ultimate humiliation, wouldn't it? My hand still rested on his shoulder, so I gave it a squeeze and moved on down the aisle. Billy had to come to the yearbook room at seventh period, the hour when his class schedule dictated that he was part of the yearbook staff, so maybe he'd get things worked out with Shirlee then.

But when seventh period came, he didn't appear. Everyone was busy—selecting photos, cropping them with grease pencils, writing captions, laying out pages. Shirlee was talking to Tim, who did the sports pages, about the photos from the homecoming game that had just come in.

"Where's Billy?" I asked loudly, wanting Shirlee to hear my concern. As I spoke, I looked all around the room as though I might locate him, perhaps hiding under one of the desks.

"He was in the nurse's office right after lunch," Tim volunteered.

"The nurse's office?" I repeated. "What was wrong with him?"

"Only about the biggest shiner I've ever seen," Tim replied with the tiniest gleam of satisfaction in his eye. "Somebody said he got into a fight with Hank Wertzler. I think they've both been suspended for the rest of the week."

"Jeez," a boy named Jim said. "Billy Simmons against Hank Wertzler? That I'd like to see!"

"I wouldn't," I protested. "Billy could have been really hurt."

But everyone laughed anyway. Even Shirlee smiled.

Did Billy have a single friend in this room?

Even me?

Billy was back in school the next Monday, but he didn't return to the staff room for seventh-period class. Someone said he must be so far behind in his classes after his time out of school that he'd had to drop the yearbook to catch up on the rest. But I knew Billy. He was a good student. Even a week on suspension couldn't put him far enough behind in his other classes that he couldn't catch up.

I tried to stop to talk to him as I was leaving study hall the next day, but he just rolled his eyes meaningfully at Mr. Morand, the gym teacher and coach in charge of the big study hall. Apparently, he was afraid he'd get into trouble for talking. And maybe he would have. Once a kid has been suspended for anything at all, some of the teachers will have it in for him anytime he blinks.

The next time I saw Billy was several days later. He was walking down the hall, with Hank and Jason on either side of him, making me wonder if he was being abducted. The pile of books pressed to his narrow chest was so big that I figured he must have been carrying theirs as well as his own. But when our eyes met, I might have been a stranger. Billy just looked right on through me and kept walking.

I turned after they had passed, staring, only to see the

tip of a small lavender book extending above the back pocket of Billy's jeans. *At least,* I consoled myself, *he still has his journal.* I wondered, though, if he was still drawing pictures of Shirlee.

All this meant that I now had my precious third-period hour alone with Shirlee every day—exactly what I'd wanted. And I can't say it wasn't precious, because it was, despite my occasional rushes of guilt about Billy. Shirlee and I talked about this and that. Sometimes I graded tests for her. More often I did extra work for the yearbook. She even gave me some of the other kids' copy to edit. The real editor was a senior, as the editor always was, and too busy with his own world of classes and girlfriends to put in the time really needed. I knew without Shirlee's ever saying so that I would be editor the next year, and I knew that nothing—absolutely nothing—would come ahead of the yearbook when *I* held the top position.

I wish I could say that I missed Billy, but the truth is I didn't. He had dropped from my consciousness almost as easily as he had dropped from the yearbook staff. And since we didn't share any classes except for the large, third-period study hall I never stayed in, I seldom saw him or thought about him. Sometimes I noted the back of his slender neck bent over a textbook in study hall, but that was all.

If my conscience troubled me occasionally, I always reminded myself that I had done nothing. How could I help what I'd seen by accidentally stepping into the force field of Billy's rapt attention? Besides, the magic of my hours now spent entirely alone with Shirlee wiped everything else away.

It was November before she invited me to her home again, this time along with two other girls from the staff, Jennifer and Cynthia, who were now in charge of the sophomore class pages. It was Friday, and we were to make popcorn balls to be sold at that evening's basketball game as a fundraiser for the yearbook. When the day came, it turned out that I was the only one who could go to Shirlee's. (To my amazement, I discovered that the other girls had decided they had something more important to do!)

Shirlee didn't complain about its being only me, though, and the two of us, working side by side, filled half a dozen grocery bags with waxed-paper-wrapped popcorn balls. When we had finished the job, we looked at each other and laughed. We both had the rapidly hardening syrup everywhere, on our hands, in our hair, even on the tips of our noses.

We cleaned up, then headed back to the school to sell our wares at the game. By the time we emerged again into the night, the world had been transformed. Sleet had turned to freezing rain, and the trees, the grass, the sidewalks, the roads shimmered beneath the streetlights like fine crystal. The world was magical, but the roads were treacherous.

"We'll never make it all the way to Osborne," Shirlee

said. "It's a good thing my house is close. You can call your folks and tell them you're staying with me."

And that was the first time I slept with Shirlee.

A student sleeping with a teacher? How could such a thing be possible? But this was, you must understand, an innocent time. When two women lived together, even spent their entire adult lives together, they were seen merely as two old maids taking what dry comfort they could in each other's company. After all, what could possibly happen between two women? Or between a woman teacher and a female student? The very idea of suspecting them of anything was ridiculous. And my careful parents certainly didn't voice any objections when I called them. Mother just sounded glad that I wouldn't be traveling home on the ice.

Everything felt awkward at first. Shirlee had only one bed, of course. After all, she lived alone. Even her sofa was too short to accommodate a sleeper. I hadn't brought pajamas or a toothbrush or any of the other necessities I would have carried to an overnight with a friend, either. But Shirlee loaned me a pair of soft flannel pajamas, even found me a new toothbrush, and we settled into the living room to eat the tag ends of the popcorn—without any syrup; we'd had enough of the sticky sweet—and to gaze out her picture window at the glittering night.

After a time Shirlee said in that matter-of-fact way of hers, "I don't know about you, but I'm bushed. Let's go to bed."

And so she climbed in on one side, and I climbed in the

other. I felt strangely cautious, as though if a finger or toe strayed across some invisible line I might be burned. We said good night, and Shirlee rolled onto her side and went immediately to sleep. I lay on my back, rigid, telling myself that spending a night in bed with Shirlee was no different, after all, than any overnight with a friend . . . except that for some reason it was a long time before I could breathe steadily, calmly enough to fall asleep.

In the middle of the night I awakened to the sound of a high-pitched, wavering whistle. It took me several heart-pounding seconds to remember where I was and to understand that what I was hearing was the snoring of my most sophisticated and beloved teacher. I lay on my side of the bed, smiling into the darkness. I couldn't have loved her more!

And so it became a regular practice, my going over to Shirlee's house, sometimes in the company of other girls, more often alone, and sometimes staying overnight when I was the only one. Her boyfriend, Dave, I learned, worked for the railroad, and when he was off on trips, Shirlee got lonely. Not that I presumed he stayed overnight at her house when he was in town. A single female teacher in the 1950s could never have survived the scandal of a male overnight guest.

And then, deep in the dark of one winter night, every-thing changed . . . though even after it did, I wasn't entirely sure what had happened. I was, once again, stay-ing overnight with Shirlee, sleeping primly on my side of the bed, when I was brought sharply awake by a warm arm stretching across my waist.

"Come here," a voice said, muffled with sleep. "Come here, little one." The arm tugged at me.

After resisting for a sleep-befuddled moment, I gave in and allowed the arm to pull me close against the body on the other side of the bed. Kisses on my forehead, my cheeks—one kiss for each—then a long, tender hug . . . then release. Shirlee turned away, sinking back into the sleep she had never left.

I lay abandoned next to her after she had turned away, my heart pounding so raucously that my breath came in gasps. And as I lay there, every muscle in my body stretched tight like a rubber band, another deeper pounding started up from that unnamed, unmentionable place between my legs.

I didn't have a clue what was happening. The sensation was so strange that I wondered if I might be dying. I almost cried out to waken Shirlee, to ask her to help me, to protect me. But something let me know that I should not.

Both poundings subsided gradually . . . gradually. Still, I lay there the rest of the night, unable to move, afraid I might touch her, longing to touch her, feeling wholly transformed, understanding and refusing to understand.

Shirlee had done nothing wrong; I was certain of that. How can anyone do wrong from a deep sleep? I had only been part of her dream. But a dream of what? Of whom? Of Dave? Certainly not. I had met him once. He was a bear of a man. She never would have called him "little one." So the dream must have been of me. *Little one?* Did she see me as a child?

And what had the pounding meant? Not the pounding of my heart, but that other deeper, more disturbing pounding. Whatever Shirlee had reached for, what she had taken into her arms was not a child. Could I tell her what had happened . . . ever?

The next morning, when Shirlee woke, I pretended to be waking, too, and lay there studying her as she sat, disheveled and, to my mind, utterly beautiful, on the edge of the bed.

"Good morning, Shirlee." I spoke softly.

She turned to offer a sleepy, completely unselfconscious smile. "Good morning, Claire," she said.

And I knew. She didn't remember! She had not the slightest notion of what had happened in the night. That she had pulled me close, that she had kissed me, that she had set off that terrifying explosion in that unnamed place down there was as remote from her awareness as the moon was from the earth.

I could never tell her about any of it. I couldn't even dare write about it in my all-too-private journal.

So that was the second secret I kept from Shirlee. The first, of course, was my sharing of Billy's crime. And eventually I would learn what power secrets have. The second secret piled on top of the first began the construction of a barrier, one behind which I discovered no recourse but to hide my truth-telling heart. And without truth, where is love?

The next Monday, I encountered Billy in the hall as I was heading downstairs for my now-private hour with Shirlee. To my surprise, he lifted a hand in response to my wave, then stopped, clearly expecting more.

He said nothing, though, so I opened with, "We miss you on the yearbook staff. I wish you hadn't dropped the class."

"Do you?" he asked. And there was a sudden hunger in his eyes when he added, "What does Shirlee say about me?"

The truth was she had said nothing, not one single word. It was as though he had never existed. But I wasn't sure whether that news would relieve him—at least it meant she wasn't badmouthing him—or make everything worse. So I said only, "She hasn't said much, certainly nothing bad."

"Yeah," he said, and the silence stretched taut between us, like the string of a musical instrument waiting to be plucked.

I looked at his stack of books. The cloth-covered lavender one wasn't on the top, but then I remembered and stepped to one side so I could check the last place I'd seen it. It was in his back pocket again. "You're still drawing in your journal?" I asked.

"No reason to stop," he replied. "I've got the same audience now that I had before." I must have looked confused, because he added, with a small, rather twisted smile, "Me."

"Oh," I said, getting, if somewhat belatedly, the dig about Shirlee's agreeing to read our journals and then not doing it. "Shirlee doesn't really have time to—" I started to say.

He stopped me with a wave of his hand, and I let my justification trail off. I still turned my journal over to Shirlee every couple of weeks, and she still returned it to me, smiling, saying, "Nice!" or something not much different from that. Once I'd even plucked a long hair from my head and laid it along one page and then folded the hair back over a later page, just to check, and when Shirlee returned the journal, the hair had not been disturbed. So I knew she hadn't so much as opened the book. That was another of my secrets, knowing she didn't read my journal but still pretending with her that she did.

"She shouldn't have told us she'd read them if she didn't have time to do it," I admitted. It was the first "bad" thing I had ever said about our beloved teacher.

"She shouldn't have," Billy agreed.

"But you still love her . . . don't you?" I almost whispered the words.

He didn't reply, only gazed down the hallway as though something fascinating had suddenly appeared there. I turned to look, but saw nothing.

"You *do*," I insisted, turning back to face him. I don't know why it mattered to me that Billy admit his feelings, but it did.

Instead of responding to my challenge, he went off on another tack. "My mom met Shirlee once," he said. "She said it was amazing, that she'd never seen such a resemblance."

"Resemblance?" I repeated, confused.

"She said Shirlee looks just like the woman who took care of me for a while when I was about three. My mom got sick, see, and had to spend weeks in the hospital, so this woman, she was my mother's friend, took me home with her until Mom got well again."

"Do you remember the woman?" I asked, wondering how we'd gotten onto this topic. "Do you think she looked like Shirlee?"

"No." Billy shook his head. "I don't remember her at all. I didn't even remember that my mom was ever sick."

"But you—" And then I stopped, understanding suddenly what he was saying. "Do you think that's what love is? I mean, all it is?"

"Just trying to recapture someone who was important to you when you were a little kid?" Billy asked.

"Yeah." Somehow the idea offended me.

Billy grinned. I could tell he was delighted that I had gotten his point. But then he spoiled everything by answering my question. "No," he said. "I don't think it's always that. With you and Shirlee, I think the attraction is pure sex."

I was so shocked that for a moment I couldn't breathe. Me and Shirlee? Sex? People didn't even use the word in 1955, let alone make accusations like that!

I didn't stay to hear more. I turned and practically ran away, the leather heels of my flats clacking in the empty hallway, covering any other charges Billy might be ready to hurl after me.

How could Billy Simmons, of all people, dare suggest such a thing? I didn't even begin to catch my breath until I had turned into the stairwell leading to the first floor.

He was jealous. That was all. That's what such ugliness had come out of. Pure jealousy.

I headed down the stairs to the yearbook room . . . to be with Shirlee. Being with her would make everything all right. Wouldn't it?

IV

It was Friday, and I was on my way home with Shirlee to spend the night again. The end of the second six-week grading period was at hand, and she had to compile grades for all her classes. I had helped her with this before. Only she could write the final grades into the report cards—they had to be in her handwriting—but I could add up the numbers from the various tests and papers and tell her what the grades should be. The whole process went pretty fast that way.

I wondered sometimes how other teachers managed to get all their paperwork done without help, but then I always reminded myself that other teachers didn't have the extra burden of the school yearbook.

I had been thinking of Billy steadily since our

encounter in the hall, thinking and burning in a quiet fury. What right did he have . . ? What right did *anyone* have deciding anything so private about me? If I were . . . well, *that way,* wouldn't I be the first to know?

What had happened with Shirlee that night didn't mean a thing. It was an odd accident, that's all, arising from the confusion of sleep. An accident on both of our parts.

"You're quiet tonight," Shirlee said, and I smiled apologetically.

"Just thinking," I told her.

"What about?" she asked.

"About more things I want to write in my journal," I said.

"Then I guess I'll have to wait to read them, won't I?" She said this cheerfully, looking right into my eyes, as though she would be reading them. And maybe she— But no. I knew better.

We finished our supper of pork chops and canned peas and Rice-a-Roni—my mother never made Rice-a-Roni, and I loved it; it was so bland and smooth in the mouth— and settled at opposite ends of the couch in the living room. I added up numbers; Shirlee wrote down the grades. It took longer to add up the numbers than to write the grades, so Shirlee was reading the jokes in a *Reader's Digest* and chuckling as she waited for me to come up with each total. It occurred to me that we could have moved faster if she would add some numbers, too, but she didn't offer to, so I put the thought aside. She had been teaching all week; she was probably tired and needed the relief of *Reader's Digest* jokes.

We had been working for a half hour or so—darkness had fallen outside—when I noticed a movement at the front curb. It wasn't a car. No one could have parked there anyway, because Dave had never gotten around to burning the leaves Billy and I had raked that fateful day. The pile had just lain there at the edge of the street, growing increasingly sodden. I had suggested on an earlier visit that we burn them, but Shirlee had said no, that they were probably too wet now to burn.

I lifted my head from my task and looked more carefully. There it was . . . someone outside . . . at the curb. And not just one person—two . . . no, three dark shapes wove in and out of one another.

"Shirlee," I said.

"Do you have Dick Schneider's grade?" she asked.

"Not yet," I said. "But look. Out front. Do you see?" I pointed toward the figures that could be clearly seen through the low picture window directly across from us.

Shirlee glanced up, then back at her magazine. "Probably just someone out walking their dog," she said.

But I didn't think so. I put the grade book aside, stood, and walked to the window.

From that vantage point I could see more clearly. Someone tall and large was bending over, pouring something . . . onto the pile of leaves? And someone else held something up. It looked like a sign, but I couldn't read it in the darkness. The third figure stood back, either watching or instructing the others.

Then it happened. Everyone stepped away, and a light flared. A match? Whatever it was, it flared and arced through the air, and suddenly the dark pile that had been nothing but damp leaves exploded. A brilliant white ball rose in the darkness. It wasn't so much that the pile of leaves was on fire, but that the very air above it burned. That quick flash of fire was followed by a smoky, mushroom-shaped cloud, as if a miniature atom bomb had been set off.

This all happened so quickly that I didn't even have time to gasp, let alone call Shirlee to my side, and it wasn't until the fire had settled back onto the pile and the three dark figures had scattered that I finally found voice to call out to her.

"Shirlee!" I cried, but she had already leapt from the couch.

"What the—?" she shouted, racing for the front door.

I followed. Outside the night was cold and entirely clear except for the smoke. The fire continued to burn—it was in the pile of leaves at the curb, as I had thought—but without much enthusiasm. Still, it gave off enough light that I could make out the sign propped in the middle of the pile. It was a long sheet of paper, the kind that comes off a roll in art class, supported by crossed sticks that must have been attached to some kind of a base. The picture on the piece of paper was of a voluptuous woman, wearing glasses, freckles, and nothing else at all. Just before the flame reached the picture and the whole thing began to wither and curl, I made out a brightly colored butterfly on the side of one breast.

I turned to look at Shirlee, wondering if she, too, had seen. She stood there, transfixed, the light from the fading fire turning her features ruddy.

"That little queer!" she said.

"Who?" I asked, stunned at the word, not wanting to believe it had come from my teacher's mouth.

"Billy Simmons. That damned little faggot. This is his work! I'd know it anywhere. I've seen those pictures he used to draw in class."

And of course, she was right. Since Billy and Hank and Jason had come to be such "good friends," those goons were probably the two with him, but only Billy could have drawn the picture. I wondered who'd come up with the idea, the hoods or Billy.

It was then that I saw something lying in the grass and bent to pick it up. A small book with a lavender cover. It must have fallen out of Billy's pocket.

Before Shirlee could see it, I tucked the journal beneath my sweater, out of sight. "But you have no proof it was Billy," I reminded her, my tone definite, even a little hard. "There's no way you can be sure."

After all, I figured we queers had to stick together.

And that's the end of my story . . . pretty much. A few minutes later I complained of not feeling well and asked Shirlee to take me to the bus stop. The grades weren't even all recorded when I left.

I continued on the yearbook staff, but I quit spending

all my study halls with Shirlee and mostly used them for studying instead. I never went home with her again.

I noticed, a couple of weeks later, that a sophomore girl on the staff was correcting papers for her during class.

I suppose it's true that I blamed Shirlee, at least for a time. For using us to do her work. For pretending to have read our journals when she hadn't. For calling Billy names.

For a time, I blamed her, too, for opening the door to a knowledge of myself I wasn't ready to possess. But then that blame was forgotten, because I closed the door almost as emphatically as it had been thrown open. I wasn't ready to know what I knew, not in 1955, when homosexuality was still classified as a mental illness, prosecuted as a crime, labeled as a sin. In the face of all that disapproval, I hadn't the courage to live my own truth. And so I put aside what I had discovered and didn't take it out again for a long, long time. Years later, when I stumbled upon the true nature of my sexuality again, I found to my astonishment that a deeply satisfying, even joyful life awaited me. I finally fit comfortably inside my own skin.

Billy left town after he graduated from high school to attend a beauty college in Chicago, and afterward he came back to our community to open his own shop. He is a fine hairdresser, I am told. He also came back with a wife, and between them, over the years, they produced three children. As far as I know, they are together still.

Which just goes to show . . . actually, I'm not entirely sure what it does go to show except that sometimes we should all reserve judgment. Sometimes, you see, everything we know—even about ourselves—is untrue.

An Afterword

These five stories are a curious—to the author, at least—amalgam of autobiography and fiction. I was the girl who grew up in the 1950s in the shadow of a cement mill on the edge of a small town in Illinois. I was the new girl in a school where I didn't belong, the betrayer of Miss Kitty, the telephone prankster and new confirmee. I was the adolescent in love with her teacher. Though each story departs from the facts of my life— some in small ways, some in large ones—each one begins with some deep truth of my own experience. In thirty years of publishing, I have never before drawn my fiction so directly from my own well.

When I was growing up, my parents taught me to hold my feelings close, never to reveal too much . . . either the positive or the negative. My mother and father loved me and worked hard to make a good life for me and my brother, but neither of them had any appreciation for the stories I wove so endlessly in my mind. All that was just part of "Marion's nonsense." And yet, despite their lack of support for or approval of my inner world, I grew into a woman who wrote stories.

What I did not grow into was a woman who wrote stories about herself, at least not in any transparent way. I am present in the more than sixty books I have published before now, of course, but only in fragments. Bits of my experience appear here, scraps of a place I've lived there, an incident with one of my pets in another story. *On My Honor* was the first of my books to be based on a real event, but it was something that happened to a friend of mine, not to me. What I have never written about directly is the girl I was. Even when I wrote something like an autobiography—*A Writer's Story*—it became what one librarian referred to as a "storiography" . . . the story of my stories, not of my life.

Perhaps I didn't write about that long-ago girl because, before I could, I needed to move far enough away from her to understand her, gather enough perspective to care about her as she deserved. And I needed, as well, to find a way of writing that could use the techniques of fiction to tell the most naked truths. Time and experience have come together to make these stories possible.

Every story here remains true to my girlhood experience. Yet from the moment I began writing the first one, I knew that fiction would be necessary in order to discover all I wanted to explore. For instance, an African-American girl named Dorinda appears as the central character in "Friend of Liberty." No such girl ever existed. The facts on which her story is based, however, are all too real.

I grew up in a totally segregated *northern* community, and two aspects of that experience made this story an important one for me to imagine and to write. One is that much has been made—is still being made—of the experience of segregation in the South. The fact that segregation when it occurred in the North was often much more ironclad than the southern version is seldom acknowledged. I wanted to say it out loud: Segregation is segregation.

The other aspect that I needed to examine was my own limitations—limitations imposed by the experience of growing up in a community where only whites were allowed. They were *my* limitations, not those of the excluded African-American community, and they were the kind of limitations that, no matter how open or well-intentioned my family might have been, inevitably produced ignorance. I emerged from my childhood knowing little that was meaningful about the entire nonwhite world. And so I created "Friend of Liberty" as a way of exploring not just the sin of segregation but also the depths of the ignorance that segregation creates in those who exclude.

The three middle stories, "New Girl," "Killing Miss Kitty," and "Sin," are all shaped out of the material of my own life. Every significant character is based on a real person from my past, renamed here. Much of what is portrayed actually happened. Nonetheless, some of the "facts" are made up or borrowed from someone else's experience, and disparate events come together to inform one another in a way they had no opportunity to do in real time.

Writing these stories would not have been possible when I was closer to the real happenings. It has taken long years to gain empathy for the awkward, self-conscious, self-critical adolescent in "New Girl," to forgive my mother's role in the death of my cat, to reconcile the burdens imposed by my church with the blessings it bestowed.

The final story, "Everything We Know," is another creation, fiction only loosely based on fact. Nearly all of the people in this story are real, though again names have been altered. Some of the events are drawn from my life; many are invented. Nonetheless, the truth revealed—a truth I chose not to face for another thirty years—stands.

"Sometimes, you see," this last story concludes, "everything we know—even about ourselves—is untrue." And sometimes our own deepest truths can best be revealed—even *to* ourselves—in stories.